SPEEDING BULLET

Other Books by Neal Shusterman

Dissidents

The Shadow Club

Kid Heroes

Neon Angel:
The Cherie Currie Story (with Cherie Currie)

S·P·E·E·D·I·N·G B·U·L·L·E·T

A NOVEL BY

NEAL SHUSTERMAN

SCHOLASTIC INC.
New York Toronto London Auckland Sydney

No part of this publication may be reproduced in whole or in part, or stored in a retrieval system, or transmitted in any form or by any means, electronic, mechanical, photocopying, recording, or otherwise, without written permission of the publisher. For information regarding permission, write to Little, Brown & Company, Inc., 34 Beacon Street, Boston, MA 02108.

ISBN 0-590-45424-2

12 11 10 9 8 7 6 5 4   4 5 6 7/9

Printed in the U.S.A.   01

First Scholastic printing, November 1992

ACKNOWLEDGMENT

I'd like to thank Lloyd Segan and Michael Haney, for their input and support.

My love and thanks to Elaine for always being there, and to Stephanie for always being right!

And a very special thanks to Tony Aliengena, the real-life boy flier who inspired the character of Bobby O'Donnell.

For Brendan,
who went to my heart
faster than a speeding bullet,
and for my father,
who will always be a superhero

SPEEDING BULLET

1 · Screaming Steel

Nick was the first one out the door, and the shriek of the three o'clock bell still echoed in the iron stairwell as he raced down. It was more than a school bell, however, that echoed through Nicholas Herrera's troubled brain today.

You have to believe in yourself, Nick's teachers had told him. Believe in himself! Teachers were always full of such wise and empty answers to all of life's problems.

Maybe there were kids somewhere who could swallow that line and believe themselves all the way into Harvard, but Nick didn't hang out with any of them.

On the first floor of Harrison High, Nick bashed through the dented steel doors. The dark, graffiti-covered doors opened up into the bright light of day. Before him a twisted knot of traffic wove down Second Avenue. Ignoring the pedestrians who were almost creamed by the school's outer door as it flew open, Nick turned the corner, and stormed up Seventy-fifth Street. A gust of wind tore down the street, blowing through the curled locks of his shoulder-length brown hair.

Behind him he heard a voice call his name, but he didn't even acknowledge it — he was too busy stewing over the D+ he had just received on his trig exam. This time it had been Old Man Carbuckle's turn to tell him that "difficulties in mathematics stem from a lack in belief in one's own abilities."

There was this conspiracy of teachers, Nick knew, and they all wanted to paint simple pictures of life — textbook solutions, where the answers were always A, B, or C. They held fast to their storybook ideals; "Good things come to those who wait." "Believe in yourself, and you'll have everything your heart desires." "Wishing will make it so."

Nick often wondered if the teachers really believed what they said, or if they said it just to make their own lives easier. Maybe they said it because it was how they *wished* the world could be.

"Hey, Nicky," said the voice, now far behind, but Nick was in no mood to deal with Marco today. Marco was the kind of guy who wouldn't shut up. He had an opinion on everything, and his opinions made about as much sense as trigonometry. He began every sentence with the words "You know what I think?" The question should have been "You *care* what I think?" but if he began his sentences that way, he would live a very quiet life.

It would have been hard for Nick to enjoy his present pissed-off mood with Marco blathering on about everything and nothing, so Nick sped up his pace up the hill of Seventy-fifth Street, down the row of brownstones until he reached Lexington Avenue.

A D+!

The tenth grade was only three weeks old, and he was already back to ground zero.

Perhaps you don't try hard enough, the school counselors would always say to him when his grades did their traditional belly flop on the rocks.

Well, perhaps they were right — but what if he *did* try harder and failed? It was better to fail by design than risk failing for real, wasn't it?

Yes, believing in *himself* was far too dangerous. When he had to believe in something, he much preferred, like his mother, to believe in God and His mysterious ways. At least there, there was some hope — at least there he wouldn't be alone in his belief.

The simple fact, Nick felt, was that some people were just plain stupid — some people simply had a million fewer living brain cells than others — and it had absolutely nothing to do with background, or where you came from. Some people, Nick believed, were just dealt a brainful of lousy cards.

Teachers hated to admit the existence of stupidity. They would look in your face and come up with a million other reasons why you weren't doing well in school. For once — just once, Nick wished a teacher would have the guts to say, "All right, you're stupid — you were born that way — you're a poor dumb slob with all the brain power of a dented Ping-Pong ball, but you know what? Just because you're stupid doesn't mean you can't *learn* how to be smart."

If a teacher just once would bag the "believe in

yourself" crap and level with him instead, maybe, just maybe, he might take the challenge and learn how to be smart. But right now, things being the way they were, he saw no good reason to go out on such a shaky limb.

There was no shame in being stupid, he knew. Stupid people were probably the backbone of civilization. All the world's nations had been built by stupid people. It always seemed to be the smart ones who ended up tearing it all down.

No, the problem was not that he was stupid — the problem was that he was stupid and *knew* it.

• • •

Lexington Avenue was a zoo, a bizarre menagerie of all forms of life, all of which seemed to be in a horn-blaring or heel-clicking hurry to be someplace else. Nick turned off Seventy-fifth, onto the busy avenue.

Across the street, construction workers clung to the ledge of a new tower probably being built by Lanko, who is the city's fastest builder. The workers shouted and whistled down at anything with long hair or a dress.

Around Nick, harried men in silk business suits brushed shoulders with overworked delivery men, and wealthy women in French fashions crossed paths with vagrants milling up and down the street, their soot-covered hands reaching out for the quarters that only tourists were likely to give.

Everyone's late.

Everyone's behind schedule,

and it's everyone else's fault.

At 3:05, on this windy October afternoon, the first wave of rush hour had begun with the opening of the school doors. Nick did not feel like fighting with hordes of kids packing themselves into the subway cars, and so he made sure he was the first one to the station. With any luck, he might have a seat all the way to Ninety-sixth Street.

"Hey, Nicky! Wait up!" It was Marco again. Relentless Marco, who would chase Nick to the ends of the earth. Nick sighed and turned to see, across the street, Marco Mednick's stocky body bump into some old Puerto Rican woman, who started spouting machine-gun Spanish at him. Marco picked up her bag, apologized, and raced across the street, ignoring the Don't Walk sign as if catching up with Nick was more important than his life.

Nick was a block ahead now and making good time, but with his anger beginning to fade, he didn't have the heart to leave Marco behind with no explanation. Marco would take it personally and be depressed for the rest of the day.

If there was any consolation to Nick, it was that his friend's mental Ping-Pong ball was more dented than his own. In fact, Marco Mednick was perhaps the stupidest being in New York City that didn't walk on four legs. His accent was so heavily Brooklynese that the untrained ear would probably need a translator to decipher it. Funny, because he'd never lived in Brooklyn — he had been brought up in the same old rent-controlled Manhattan building as Nick.

Marco was truly one of the lucky, for he was stupid in the right way. Marco was stupid, but didn't know it.

Nick was sure Marco would live a happy (if somewhat dim) life. He would marry some jolly stupid woman, and have kids who were stupid-squared. A relative would slip him into some job that required more brawn than brain. He would go on strike every three years for ten cents more per hour, and eventually buy a home in Staten Island, where he could watch TV and blame all the world's problems on the Japanese, the mayor, or his kids. His would be a wonderful life.

Like Nick, Marco had a mix-and-match ancestry, but Marco's wasn't as well defined as Nick's half-Italian, half–Puerto Rican lineage. Marco was a human melting pot. He was remotely Armenian, distantly Italian, slightly Scandinavian, questionably Hispanic, somewhat WASPish, but had a Jewish last name that no member of his family could trace. Somewhere in the world, Marco must have had relatives with all the good genes from the family's multinational background. But none of these relatives lived in New York.

While Nick was tall for his age, and managed to pull out some decent looks, Marco had missed the boat on both counts. He compensated for it by building up miraculous muscles in his upper body, but forgot his lower body. So now he had Arnold Schwarzenegger's chest, resting on Pee-wee Herman's legs.

Still, Marco was a great guy, and perhaps the most loyal friend Nick had ever had. He was more like a brother than Nick's own brothers were, and Nick couldn't just leave him behind today — even if it meant missing an empty train.

Sweaty and out of breath, Marco finally caught up

with him. "You know what I think?" said Marco. "I think you got some bug up your butt, and it's eatin' your brain! What the hell are you movin' so fast for? Din-cha hear me cawlin' you?"

"I heard you."

"So?"

"So, let's hurry to the subway before every snot-nosed kid and their brother hog all the seats."

Marco agreed, and they strode off toward the Seventy-seventh Street station. Nick figured Marco knew what was behind Nick's bad mood, because they sat right next to each other in math class.

"You flunk it?" asked Marco, as they climbed down the steps into the dark station.

"D-plus."

"Oh," said Marco. "I flunked it."

"A D-plus isn't exactly passing."

"Better than an F. Hey, you know what I think? I think Old Man Carbuckle has it in for us. I think he's queer, too."

Nick laughed. Marco had two distinctions of people in addition to male and female — that was "queer" and "not-queer." Anyone Marco liked was not-queer. Anyone he didn't had to be queer. Accord-to Marco, nine-tenths of Harrison High School was homosexual.

The Seventy-seventh Street IRT subway station served its purpose, and not much more. It was not a thing of beauty. The concrete platform was almost black from age-old chewing gum and tobacco stains. The steel girders holding up the city above had been painted over dozens of times, and psychedelic patterns of colors formed whenever they started to peel.

Nick dropped his token into the turnstile, and

Marco followed, jabbering on about bad grades and teachers' sexual preferences.

Today Nick had not been fast enough. The platform before them was packed with businessmen and uniformed students from some nearby Catholic school.

At the edge of the tunnel, the bright headlight of the train lit up the girders, and the train tore through the station a moment later, the brakes letting off a bloodcurdling steel scream as they labored to bring the Lexington Avenue Local to a halt. No one much cared about the noise — it was something everyone had grown accustomed to.

People near the platform edge barely flinched as the train barreled past them at fifty miles an hour. It was something else they'd grown accustomed to. Only out-of-towners stood back, holding their ears and marveling at the way New Yorkers practically played chicken with the leading edge of a speeding train.

The train screamed itself to an exhausted stop, and the doors rattled open to reveal a crowded human mosaic. Marco cursed beneath his breath. Each car was packed, leaving barely any room for breathing. It reminded Nick of the old trick of cramming people into a telephone booth.

Through the open door and windows, he could see dozens of hands reaching up to hold the steel rings for support. The rest just stood in the middle, safely buffered by hundreds of tightly packed bodies.

In the station, the masses pushed their way across the yellow line at the edge of the platform and into the doors. Defying the laws of physics, they managed to find room to stand.

Nick was not about to force his way into this tin can. After all his effort, he'd have to wait for the next train.

Nick sighed. "You can't win."

Marco shook his head in agreement. "You know what *I* think?" said Marco. "I think there's too many people movin' into Manhattan, and it's gonna get too heavy, so's it's gonna make us have an earthquake." He shook his head and glanced up at the girders holding up the city above them. Then he added, "It's the mayor's fault."

Nick had to smile.

"What's so funny?" defended Marco. "It's true — my mom read it in the *Post*." That made Nick laugh even harder. Marco's mom would also believe the earth was flat if she read it in the *New York Post*.

The doors closed, tightly clamping the dress hem of a fat woman whose rear end was just barely inside the train. The train lurched once, and then roared out of the station, the little flap of pink fabric fluttering with the breeze like a tiny flag as it went down the tunnel.

The roar echoed into the distance, and silence filled the dim station.

"Let's go," said Nick, with a flick of his head, and the two sauntered down the platform, to the very end of the station. The front car of the next train would stop way up there, and the front car was usually the least crowded.

On the way Nick, as was his habit, pulled a nickel out of his pocket and began casually flipping it, letting his mind drift in and out of the girders of the station.

His earlier anger was resolving itself into a dull

acceptance of his academic lot. He had thought this year would be different because he had started with a positive attitude. He had even dreamed of freaking everyone out by pulling in A's on his first report card, but now that dream was shot to hell. The chances of Marco's great metropolitan weight-quake were greater.

Nick wondered just how much more defeat he could stand before he would bail out of the respectable world, the way his older brother, Salvatore, had. Salvatore's solution to life's problems had been to turn bad — and Nick's mom had this annoying habit of telling Nick how much he was like Salvatore.

But since Salvatore was no longer around, there wasn't much basis for comparison, was there?

"Hey, Marco," said Nick, as they reached the far end of the station. "What are you gonna do if you don't graduate?"

"Who, me?" said Marco with empty eyes.

"No, Mother Teresa."

Marco shrugged. "Dunno," he said. "Ain't given it much thought. My dad says he could help get me a job on the docks. My uncle might get me a job as a garbage man — they do pretty good, ya know?"

"And what if you *do* graduate?" Nick asked.

"Probably pretty much the same."

Nick nodded. For Marco it didn't matter. But somehow for Nick it did. Nick knew he probably wouldn't go on to college — too many things keeping him back — but it seemed a high school degree didn't buy very much anymore, unless you had union connections like Marco did.

As they waited for the train, Nick's coin flipped up and down off his thumb and into his palm. He never bothered to check what side it landed on; he just slid it back to his thumb and flipped it again. Marco grabbed it once, but seeing Nick wasn't in a playful mood, he gave it back to him without a word. Nick continued flipping as he leaned back against the sticky green girder. He thought of pulling out a comic book from his pack to read, but felt too lazy to do it.

The station was beginning to fill up now. All sorts of people stood on the platform down toward the entrance, and very few of them came as far down as Nick and Marco were. Just a couple of blue "suits," and a student or two. Farther down, a poorly dressed man with a scraggly beard staggered to the edge of the platform, stuck his head out, and peered down the tunnel for a hint of the train, then staggered back into the crowd.

A woman with half a dozen new shopping bags walked toward Nick and Marco with her young daughter following behind, playing blue-bird-blue-bird-through-my-window around the girders.

"Hey," said Marco, after the long silence, "maybe my dad or uncle could help you get a job, too. We could work together." He was trying to be helpful, but it only made Nick feel worse.

"Thanks, Marco," said Nick, trying to hide what he was really feeling. Is this what he was cut out for? Dock work and hauling garbage?

He wasn't like Marco — Marco's mental wiring was just right. It was a closed circuit that functioned fine, but Nick was seriously miswired — he knew it had to be true. God had made some weird circuitry mistake in his head, because Nick knew his dreams far outreached his ability to ever achieve them. He wondered if having high-voltage dreams in a low-voltage brain would cause him to pop a major blood vessel sooner or later.

No sign yet of the uptown local.

The coin flipped up and down.

At last, far down the tunnel, a single headlight broke the darkness, reflecting off the rails that stretched into the station. It was still a minute or two away; not even the rumble of the train could be felt in the station.

It was then that the weird feeling came.

The murmurs around him became muted, as if there were too much wax in his ears. He began to feel a bit light-headed, as if not enough air were being pumped down into the station. He took a deep breath, filling his lungs with the sickly warm subway air. It left a dry and unpleasant taste in his mouth.

He watched the coin flip off his thumb and spin through the air.

Up ahead, the spotlight grew in the tunnel. The station began to rumble with the power of the approaching train.

The coin came down spinning so fast it seemed to be a solid silver ball. Nick grabbed at it and, for the first time he could remember, his hand closed on empty air. The coin slid down the back of his knuckles, slipping off toward the ground.

It was as if time had hiccuped, missed a beat, and Nick was suddenly syncopated between the seconds.

The acrid taste in his mouth had moved to the back of his throat, nearly making him gag. The feeling slid down his throat and into the hollow of his stomach, where the sound of the approaching train rumbled. It could have been a lack of oxygen, or a bad piece of lunch meat, but it felt like something else. Something much more important.

The coin twisted head over tail as it slipped to the floor. Landing on its edge, it spun for a moment like a dying top. It weaved in and out randomly before it keeled over, on the very edge of the platform, right in the middle of the yellow caution line. It clattered itself silent, showing heads.

Thomas Jefferson lay on the yellow line like a dead fish, and somehow that tiny Jefferson face seemed to trip something in Nick — some circuit breaker — and he didn't know why.

Nick intuitively knew something horrible was going to happen, even before he saw the danger with his own eyes, and that knowledge was horrifying.

On the yellow line Thomas Jefferson began to vibrate with the rumble of the train.

Nick turned to see, less than ten feet away, the little girl playing tightrope on the same yellow line. Beyond her, a few hundred yards down the tunnel, the train barreled forward.

Nobody noticed but Nick.

Everyone seemed to be buried in his or her own thoughts. Even the girl's mother was occupied, trying to fit all of the day's shopping into one Macy's bag. When she finally looked up, her daughter was teetering on the edge of the platform.

"Katie!" she yelled.

The girl spun at the force of her mother's voice, and that's all it took. In an instant, her imaginary tightrope gave way, and she fell five feet to the train tracks, landing diagonally across the cutting edge of the first rail.

The mother screamed, but her feet were glued.

The train crashed into the light of the station, the steel scream of its brakes piercing the ears of the subway travelers like a siren.

Now other people were shouting as well. One man turned away in terror, unable to look.

What happened next had nothing to do with bravery — it was instinctual. Someone had to go after the little girl, and no one was going, and so Nick had no choice in the matter. He was across the yellow caution line and falling to the tracks before his brain could register just what the hell he had done.

He hit hard, smashing his knee on a soot-black railroad tie. The little girl was screaming, but with no tears — there was not yet time for tears.

The train was past the first staircase of the two-block-long station. With his shin resting across the rail, the vibration jarred Nick so hard he thought his teeth would be rattled out of his head.

Now, with the blinding headlight less than thirty yards away, there seemed to be nothing left in the whole universe but the train, the little girl, and him.

Instantly balanced, and instantly in position, he put his hands on the girl's waist and picked her up with his strong arms . . . and hands seemed to reach out of heaven to grab the girl and lift her to the safety of the platform.

Nick was not going to be so lucky.

He turned his head to see the growing shape ahead of him, a square with a curved top — the shape of a tombstone — hurtling toward him. In the front window, he could see the conductor, his face contorted in horror that must have equaled Nick's.

Up above, the hands had disappeared, and although a million voices seemed to scream out at him, he knew that the people on the platform who had taken the little girl were not coming back for him.

He was one-on-one with the monstrous thing before him, and if he were going to live, he would have to play limbo with a speeding train.

He threw his hands and legs out straight, and came down on his chest. Now it wouldn't be the front of the train that got him like a fly on a windshield; it would be the spinning blades of the wheels.

The searing spotlight flew over his head. The unbearable squeal and rumble raced through and over him, as loud as anything he had ever heard.

Pain shot through his right arm. The wheels of the beast above him had locked, and sparks flew from the rail into his face. He closed his eyes and waited for it all to be over.

Then the squeal and rumble died, moving together into a hiss and a single heavy rattle as the train stopped. All that remained now was an unbearable ringing in his ears.

His face was down, his lips and teeth in the wet grime of the filthy ditch between the first and second rail. He felt like part of the black soot, crushed beer cans, and cellophane wrappers that bred the world's next generation of bacteria. He kept his face down in this metropolitan ooze, too frightened to lift his head, for fear that the train's hidden limbo bar could still come slicing across his neck.

He finally turned his head to the side, to see what remained of his right arm. The pain he was feeling made it clear to him that he did not have a right arm anymore. There was blood — a great deal of it. His hand lay a few inches from his face, but the pain at his elbow made it impossible to tell whether or not the hand was still attached to his body . . . unless he tried to move his fingers. So he tried.

The fingers moved up and down, perfectly under control.

Out beyond the train wheel beside him, Nick could see the area underneath the platform. No severed limbs there, just cans and cartons and cigarette butts in more of the primordial ooze that filled the places no one ever goes. In the midst of the ooze sat a rat so used to the screaming trains it had not been frightened away. It regarded Nick with professional interest, like a film critic in an empty theater. The rat didn't bother Nick — on the contrary, Nick was grateful that he was still alive to see one.

Now tears were finally coming to Nick's eyes, his emotions at last catching up with real time. He pulled in his arm, to discover a gash running from his elbow down most of his forearm.

The ringing had faded in his ears, and now he could hear screams and cries from the platform above. He could hear Marco calling his name.

A few yards ahead of him, Nick saw a bar of light stretching across the dark tracks; it was the space in between subway cars. Ignoring the pain in his arm, he began to crawl arm-over-arm in the ditch, like a soldier in the trenches, until he made it to the light. As he did, he kept spitting, trying to clear his mouth of the subway gook. He refused to press his tongue to the roof of his mouth, for fear of tasting whatever it was he was trying to spit out.

Nick stood between the two cars. His body readily obeyed when he asked it to stand, although his knee was swollen and it popped as he flexed it. Stepping on the first rail, he poked his head up, eye-level with the platform.

What he saw reminded him of a scene in *The Adventures of Tom Sawyer,* a book he had read in English last year. Now he knew how Tom and Huck must have felt when they walked in on their own funeral.

Twenty feet away, a policeman and conductor were on the scene, yelling at the rubbernecking crowd, warning them to stay back.

"Nick!" Marco kept yelling, looking under the train. Everyone probably figured Marco was just an idiot in shock and did not yet realize that Marco was the only one who had the right idea.

The policeman and conductor busied themselves controlling the crowd — anything to delay dealing with what they were sure lay on the tracks beneath them.

It seemed Marco was the only one with the right idea.

"Hey, Marco," he said in a gravelly voice, "over here!"

Heads snapped around to see him. Shouts of "He's alive!" and "Oh's" and finally cheers came from the crowds. Feet ran toward him, and hands reached down from heaven once more. The strong arms of the conductor and policeman grabbed his wrists and lifted him up from the metropolitan ooze.

The instant they grabbed his arms, Nick had a strange feeling, and he knew — just as he had known the little girl was going to fall to the tracks — that the missing wire had finally bridged the troubled circuit in his head.

There was a place and a purpose for him. There was a path about to unfold before his eyes — he knew it beyond a shadow of a doubt. And when he was lifted out from under the Lexington Avenue Local train, and onto the subway platform, he was lifted up into a whole other world.

2 · On the
Fifty-fifth Floor

On the high floors of Manhattan's midtown towers, you can't feel the rumble of the subway. You can't feel much of anything — just the slight sway of the building on windy days, the brush of the wind as it whistles up and down elevator shafts and through air-conditioner vents, and the tension of static electricity in the dry, recirculated air.

On the high floors of the midtown towers, even the distant street sounds are deadened. The muffled noises lose their sense of direction as they bounce off the smooth glass faces of the neighboring skyscrapers.

As a child, Linda would stand on her terrace and marvel at the way the horn blasts of ships came from the office tower across the street, and never from the direction of the East River, where the ships actually sailed.

Linda shared the huge apartment — which could scarcely be called an apartment — with her father, and four servants who performed any task a person could ever require. The penthouse filled the entire top floor of the pale-lavender marble and soft-peach glass skyscraper. Perhaps it wasn't the tallest in the city, or even the tallest in midtown, but it definitely was the tallest on Sutton Place — and it was the only pale-lavender marble and soft-peach glass building in the entire city. Her own bedroom had a breathtaking view of the East River and of the dark girders of the Fifty-ninth Street Bridge.

Linda sat on the floor, digging her toes into the plush alpaca rug in the living-room. Her school papers were strewn across the polished stone coffee table. She much preferred to do her homework in her study room — which had a western view, and brought in beautiful sunsets through her soft-peach windows — but when there was a boy over, her father insisted they stay in the more public rooms of the penthouse, in plain view. She obliged him, because she wouldn't put it past her father to install hidden video cameras in key locations of the house if he stopped trusting her. He was the sort of person who simply needed to know what everybody was up to at every hour of the day — especially those close to him. Linda had become very good at making him feel as if he knew everything.

"Manifest Destiny?" questioned Linda.

Across the coffee table, her boyfriend, Kyle, closed his eyes and began to recite in dull monotony. "Manifest Destiny: The expansionist belief in the mid-eighteen hundreds that the United States was destined to spread across the entire North American continent, and beyond."

He went on to talk about it for at least five minutes. She could barely hear him over the television voices that boomed through the speakers of her stereo.

"Did I get all of it?" asked Kyle, when he was done.

"Who coined the term?" asked Linda.

Kyle ran his fingers nervously through his thick blond hair and looked down, biting his lower lip. 'I'm not good with names," he said.

"You fail," she said playfully, knowing that Kyle would take it the wrong way and worry about it for the rest of the night. His reactions were as predictable as the settings of a washing machine. She could make him feel any emotion just as easily as she could put her blouses on spin-dry.

"We won't need to know that for the test, will we?" he asked, beginning to squirm.

Linda had concluded that the most interesting part about going out with Kyle was watching him squirm. And to think she had spent a large portion of last year trying to get him away from Dina Mitchell — the only other junior at Bollinger Academy with red hair and green eyes. Kyle was star of the soccer team — true, their school lost every game, but he was still the star. He got straight A's, and came from a long, long line of Harvard graduates. He was so "perfect" even Linda's father approved of him, which was scary.

Although there were many more important things than boys in Linda's life, she took a certain amount of pride in having nuked Dina Mitchell so effectively. It had been more fun than any of her actual dates with Kyle.

"John L. O'Sullivan published it in 1845, in the *United*

States Magazine and Democratic Review," said Linda, freeing Kyle from his nervous suspense. "We probably won't be tested on it, but it's good to know," she said. Kyle breathed a sigh of relief. So predictable.

As Kyle rustled though his notes, looking for a question to quiz Linda on, Linda began to rap her fingernails on the table, pretending to be impatient. Linda's were good fingernails. She took care of them, painting them with clear polish — clear because she thought pink, or red, or blue was simply too gaudy. There were girls in school who painted their nails two-tone and put glitter and tiny little beads on them. Linda preferred to keep it more elegant. She felt the same way about her jewelry — she wore just a little, to accent her appearance, not bury it.

Kyle excitedly dug through his pages, still trying to find something they hadn't already gone over, and Linda, bored to death with her studies, turned her gaze to the television. A reporter was describing some subway rescue.

The face of the boy who had performed the rescue came on the screen. He looked to be about her age, with curly brown hair that was just a bit too long, light eyes, and a dark complexion still full of its summer tan. It was an interesting face. She turned to catch Kyle's eyes, just as he looked away from her.

Kyle was jealous.

This was no news; Kyle would be jealous of a statue if Linda stared at it for too long.

"He's cute," said Linda, with a devilish grin. "Don't you think he's cute?"

Kyle didn't look up at her; he just flipped through his notes. "I don't think guys are cute," he said. Squirm, squirm, squirm.

"Oh," said Linda. "Well, if you were a girl, you'd probably think he was."

"Annexation of New Mexico," said Kyle with a touch of competitive anger in his voice — the kind of anger he had when he played soccer, which gave him just enough competitive edge to feel exceptionally miserable each time his team lost.

"August, 1846," said Linda, annoying Kyle with her quick response. She returned her gaze to the TV. The boy with the interesting face was gone, and now someone was reporting on a street fair. There was always a street fair going on somewhere.

"I can't study with all this noise!" said Kyle. He dug beneath his papers for the remote control and clicked off the TV.

Linda stretched her neck, and with both hands lifted her long copper hair back over her shoulders. The kink in her neck told her she had pored over her notes long enough.

"Kyle," she said, "we've studied our brains out. We'll both get A's — you know it and I know it, and the whole class probably knows it. So why don't you say we take a break?" It made perfect sense to her. Perhaps they could go out and get some pizza — anything but study, or talk about soccer.

Kyle shrugged and said softly, "I want an A-plus."

Linda leaned back against the sofa and let out a monumental sigh. As she rubbed her eyes, she could hear Kyle flipping pages, silently studying to himself. *That's what you get,* thought Linda, *when you have the perfect boyfriend.* Perfect boyfriend, perfect home, perfect school. It was enough to make her sick.

Linda grabbed her toes, stretching slowly down toward them, as she had learned in dance class. The slight strain in her back felt good, and when she sat straight again, her toes tingled. If she sat there long enough, staring at Kyle, she could probably make herself feel quite numb, and then she could close her eyes, for a moment, forgetting everything around her.

On this high floor, in her midtown tower, Linda could lose herself, and feel nothing when she wanted to. Nothing but the slight sway of the building. Nothing but the brush of the wind whistling through the air-conditioner vent. Nothing but the static electricity in the dry air around her.

But never, ever the rumble of the subway.

3 · A Little Bit Touched

Farther uptown, the low-rise apartment buildings stood like toadstools in the shadows of a growing high-rise forest. Slowly but surely, the view from Nick Herrera's uptown apartment was being carved away by Lanko Terrace Tower, which had sprouted up across Ninety-fifth Street practically overnight. Right now it was still just a thirty-story skeleton, void of tinted glass or colored marble. It wouldn't be long, though, before the tower was completed, and Nick's view was gone forever. Martin Lanko built his glorious towers fast and furiously, and Nick's view was a small thing compared to progress as planned by one of New York's master builders. Nick couldn't take it personally, although sometimes he did.

Nick's apartment building was not a Lanko masterpiece. It was a five-story walk-up, just like all the other walk-ups on the street, full of working-class families who refused to move from their rent-controlled homes. They were not slums, but they weren't too pretty either. The stones were turning black with age, and the cement around the cornerstones always seemed to have a faint smell of urine.

On Sunday afternoon, Nick sat on the roof, by the stairwell, watching his nineteen-year-old brother, Paulie, and Marco alternate on the bench press they kept up there. Nick, whose arm was covered with twenty-six stitches, was doing no weight-lifting today, so he read a comic book instead; the new adventures of the *Steroid Avenger of Death*.

A cool wind blew. Leaves that had fallen early from the sparse sycamore trees blew up the brick face, landing on the roof. Nick buttoned his jacket against the chill.

It had been five days since the rescue, and this was his first day out of the house since. Whatever had been down there in the subway ooze had taken root in his body, and less than six hours after his magnificent rescue, his temperature flew to 104 degrees and stayed there for three days.

"You know what *I* think?" said Marco. "I think you got a raw deal." Marco stood just behind Paulie, who labored to hoist the barbell fifteen times.

"I mean," said Marco, "if the mayor says he's gonna meet you, he should meet you. You got a raw deal."

"I thought you *did* meet the mayor," said Paulie, dropping the heavy barbell into its cradle with a clatter.

Nick shook his head, and rubbed his sore knee, which seemed to be healing much faster than his arm. "I was going to meet him, but I got sick, and then he went out of town. They said I could meet the deputy mayor, though."

"So, are you gonna meet him?"

"I don't think so," said Nick. "On account of he just got indicted."

"Indicted for what?" asked Paulie.

"Who knows?" said Nick. "Same thing they always get indicted for."

Nick turned a page in his comic book; the Steroid Avenger threw a flying dropkick at an evil thug, whose face exploded.

"Face it, you missed the boat, Nicky," said Paulie, as Marco took his place on the bench press.

Paulie was the brain of the family and was big on laying out the bottom line on any situation, no matter how cold and callous it was. Nick hated to admit it, but Paulie was right. Now that he was well enough to reap some glory, no one cared. The phone had stopped ringing. Friends had stopped calling. Newspapers and magazines had moved on to other things. It was back to life as usual for the rest of the world.

But not for Nick. For Nick, things were different now. He was sure of it.

"Somebody recognized me this morning while I was working the McDonald's counter," offered Nick.

"No kiddin'," said Marco.

"Yeah, she stopped right in the middle of her order and told me that I oughta get a medal or something."

"And what did you say to her?" asked Paulie.

Nick pursed his lips. "I said, 'You want fries with that?'"

Nick couldn't look Paulie in the eye after that.

"Did she?" asked Marco.

Nick opened his comic book again. While the Steroid Avenger poured molten lava on an enemy army, Paulie raved on and on about all the people he had read about in the news over the past year. He couldn't remember the name of anyone who had done a good deed.

"People have a very short memory," said Paulie, "unless, of course, you screw up — then people remember forever, don't they?"

Paulie didn't have to say anything else for Nick to know that he was talking about Salvatore. People remembered the bad, all right. Nick and Paulie had been forced to wear Salvatore's memory to school like an ugly tie every day for five years, and while Paulie had escaped to the anonymity of New York University, Nick was still singled out by high-school teachers who had taught Salvatore. On the first day of class they would glare at Nick, expecting only the worst from him, and they were never surprised if that was what they got.

Nick put down his tattered comic book, stood, and pulled out a coin, flipping it deftly over and over again as he sauntered toward the stairs.

"Take Dad," Paulie offered as his prime example. "He works all his life on the force, and he's *still* out on the road, getting shot at every day. Do they give him the money he deserves? No! And how many dozens of lives has he saved? How many good deeds has he done?"

"Cops are supposed to do good deeds," said Nick, still flipping his coin, and watching it land. As he neared the stairs, Nick caught the coin and held it firmly in his fist, feeling the edge press against the tendons of his palm. "They won't forget *me*," he said.

"You know what *I* think?" said Marco, but Nick went down the stairs before Marco could tell him.

•   •   •

Down in his third-floor apartment, no sooner did Nick turn on the TV than his mother came racing into the room, and plugged a thermometer into his mouth. "If you're normal, you can go to school tomorrow," she said.

Nick pressed Play on the VCR, and sat down. He accidentally banged his bandaged arm against the arm of the sofa, and cursed beneath his breath. Rose-Marie Herrera regarded her son's arm from a distance.

"You're gonna get a scar!" she said, shaking her head. "I know you're gonna get a scar."

"Bur up wur't be uh bug wrm," said Nick. *"Dockrr sub."*

"I don't care what the doctor said," answered his mom, as she closed the curtains to keep the late afternoon sun from assaulting Nick's eyes. "A scar is a scar," she said, "whether it's a bad one, or not. You don't need a scar like that."

The videotape began to run. It was the Channel Seven News report of his rescue, taped five nights ago.

"How are you feeling?" she asked.

"Murch butter," said Nick.

She left the room, only to return a few moments later to whip the thermometer out of his mouth.

"You're normal," she said, relieved. "You know, you're lucky you didn't get hepatitis," she said for the ten-thousandth time. Then she turned to the TV to see the Channel Seven reporter interviewing the little girl whom Nick saved and the girl's mother.

"You're watching this again?"

Nick shrugged. "Sure, why not?" He had watched it at least two dozen times already. At first it had been something to do. Now it was something he needed to do. Like flipping the coin.

"How many times you gonna watch it?" complained his mother.

"Shut up, Ma, this is my favorite part." Nick came onto the screen, with dirt still on his face, wearing the first set of heavy bandages on his arm. He told the reporter how easy it had been to save the little girl. "Saving myself was the hard part," he had said, with a big smile for the camera.

"Such a ham!" muttered his mother.

When the report was finished, Nick stopped it, and rewound it to the beginning. His mother shook her head, picked up a rag, and dusted off the television screen. "I don't know, Nicky; watching that thing so much . . . It's unhealthy."

The tape began to play again, and his mother gazed at the TV and at Nick with what seemed to be pity. It pissed Nick off.

"Ma," said Nick, "in case you forgot, I'm a hero — not a criminal."

She came over to him and, as she always did, gently brushed a lock of his hair out of his face.

"The cemetery's full of heroes too, Nicky," she said softly, then she turned to leave. "Next time, let someone else do it."

• • •

When the moon finally disappeared behind the skeleton tower across the street, Nick knew that sleep simply wasn't coming tonight. That was at two in the morning.

Now it was four. He had tried to lull himself to sleep by listening to the sounds of the city. The night was always filled with the hushed moan of buses, the whispered roar of jets coming into La Guardia Airport, and the occasional wail of distant sirens. These sounds had always been comforting to Nick; they gave depth and texture to the city, the way crickets and rustling leaves did to a country night. But tonight, the city played on and on, not bringing Nick any closer to sleep, and by now Nick's exhaustion had burned itself out like his fever. So he sat in the corner of his bed, waiting.

In his room, the dim streetlight painted everything in grainy black and white. The room seemed smaller in the dark, and if Nick stared long enough, he could swear he could see the walls moving closer. Across the street, the skeletal tower seemed to move closer too. It seemed as if the city itself was closing in around Nick — and he occasionally dreamed of waking up only to find his window and door closed in with cinder blocks, permanently sealing him into the brickwork of the city.

Nick knew this was what Salvatore had been fighting against: being cemented in. Perhaps that's why Salvatore was always so angry. Salvatore had been filled with an evil and desperate anger, and that's what had destroyed him. That and the gunshot.

Up until now, when Nick pictured his future he saw himself getting just as angry, just as desperate, and just as stupid as his oldest brother had been. He could see his own pitiful end.

Now, however, he saw a flip side, and it was glorious.

So he waited. At four in the morning on a sleepless night there was nothing much to do but wait for dawn, but as Nick sat there, he began to feel that he was waiting for something more.

There was an excitement growing in Nick he had never experienced before. A feeling of elation so tightly woven with a sense of fear that the two emotions became one and the same. Nick imagined this must be how people felt the first time they sky-dived — and now, that same tangled twine of fearful excitement weaved in and out of Nick's mind, tailoring him a brand new way of looking at his life. He looked at his hands — those hands that never did much besides get into an occasional fight — now they had saved a life. He had never before stopped to think what those hands could accomplish.

"All things that happen, happen for a reason," his mother always said, and she went to church often enough to know about such things. "There is no coincidence; there are no accidents; there is only a plan." If this were so, then it was clear that Nick's luck had changed — and how could he ever go back to pushing french fries, or slaving over mathematical equations he'd never understand? Opportunity was shining from a different direction entirely.

Dawn broke suddenly and the room was washed in a dim pale blue in a matter of minutes. To Nick, the sun always rose in the west, for his window only caught a reflection of dawn glancing off the brown-glass tower up on Third Avenue. Soon, a sliver of amber light cut across the old poster on Nick's closet door — a comics poster signed by some of the actual artists at a convention he had attended half a lifetime ago. Back when reading and collecting comics had been an intense hobby for him, not just a nasty habit he knew he should have outgrown.

The light cut across the face of the man of steel, the caped crusader, the Steroid Avenger, and half a dozen other imaginary superheroes. They brought back a time when Nick would spend hours fantasizing about what life would be like if he were faster than a speeding bullet, able to leap tall buildings in a single bound. Fantasies like that never really die; they just lapse into the deepest of comas.

"Everything happens for a reason," his mother always said. It was no accident he rescued the girl from the train, of that he was certain. Not because of the eerie feeling he had, and not because he had handled the rescue so well — those things could be explained.

But there was one thing that could not be explained.

It was the thing with the coins.

He hadn't told anyone about it, because everyone would think he was raving mad — but it was something he could see with his own eyes, and he knew it had to be more than just blind chance.

• • •

"Estás bien, hijo?" Nick's father's voice was barely a whisper. *"No puedes dormir, eh?"* He only spoke Spanish to Nick when he knew Nick's mother couldn't

hear — for fear that she would start conversations with Nick in Italian in retribution. Nick knew enough of both languages to answer simple questions, and carry on something like a conversation, but he chose to always answer in English. It was his way of not playing favorites.

"No, I couldn't sleep all night," answered Nick.

His father nodded in understanding and said no more about it. "You wanna come into the kitchen," he asked, "have some coffee with me before I go? Maybe some eggs?"

"OK," said Nick. He rarely got up early enough to eat with his father on weekdays, or late enough to eat with him on weekends. His father staggered toward the kitchen with a slight limp. His limp was always worse in the morning. Nick slowly slid out of bed, feeling his sweaty T-shirt clinging to his back. He peeled it off, put on a clean one, and threw on a pair of dirty jeans.

The appliances in the kitchen were old — almost ancient. White Westinghouse things with fat rounded edges, from an era before the sleek, hard look of modern-day hardware. His parents were just that way, and Nick was amazed that they even had gotten a VCR or a microwave.

It was all right, though. The old appliances had a warmth and personality to them — and they reminded Nick of his childhood, the days when he was too young and ignorant to know he was stupid.

The old percolator happily gurgled away and the rich coffee aroma filled the kitchen, smelling a million times better than coffee could possibly taste. That and the smell of frying eggs would have been enough to wake Paulie, if he hadn't been out till all hours of the night. As for Mom, well, she had long since given up trying to rise with her husband. In fact, there was rarely a morning when they ever saw each other.

As Nick devoured a runny fried egg, his father poured coffee for both of them. Nick dumped in a couple of heaping teaspoons of sugar.

"Mom says I'll have a scar," mentioned Nick, as they drank.

His father swallowed a big gulp of hot coffee. "So? Big deal." Unconsciously, he began to rub his chest, where a scar from Vietnam stretched diagonally across his breast. There was also a bullet scar on his leg. He got that while on patrol a few blocks away.

"Scars are good things," he said. "They're proof that you've lived, eh?" He downed his black coffee and poured himself another cup. Nick sipped his, the strong bittersweet taste hitting his tongue sharply.

"You don't need to meet the mayor," said his father. "When you've got a scar like that, that's the only medal you need."

He kept his eye on Nick, searching his face. Nick looked away.

"Something else is bothering you," said his father. It wasn't a question; it was a statement of fact.

"Naah," said Nick, but the lie was so blatant, he figured the old appliances would speak up and challenge him on it, if his father didn't.

Nick looked around the room, not wanting to catch his father's gaze now. The kitchen was sparsely decorated, and almost everything he could see had some sort of religious significance. That was his mother's touch. Nick had been in and out of each room in the house so often, he had just stopped seeing all the "things" on the walls, and knickknacks on shelves. On the wall above the kitchen table hung the Lord's Prayer painted on a piece of fabric so old it looked like the Shroud of Turin. On the shelf above the sink were plastic Jesuses and a Saint Christopher thermometer, shoved in among the seashells and vacation souvenirs. By the kitchen entrance was an electric clock with Jesus' face on it that emanated blue and white light from his eyes and from the halo around his head.

Well, Nick often had to remind himself that it really wasn't his mom's fault. Tacky taste was just an illness of her generation; Nick had come to the conclusion that good taste simply didn't exist before he was born.

Perhaps Nick's mother thought the constant presence of the Lord in their home would instill a sense of Catholicism in the hearts of her three sons. It still hadn't occurred to her that it was very difficult for any of them to take a glowing plastic Jesus clock seriously.

It was her devotion, and not her knickknacks that Nick took seriously — seriously enough to give up Coca-Cola or hamburgers or movies for Lent every year of his life, even though he wasn't yet sure what he truly believed.

"Dad," Nick finally asked, "now this is gonna sound strange — I mean, *real* strange coming from me. . . ."

"Yeah?"

Nick dumped the sugar from the bottom of his coffee cup into his mouth, and stalled for as long as humanly possible. Then he reached across the table for one of the quarters his mother kept in a saucer for the Laundromat. He began to flip it up and down nervously. He could feel his face flushing — something it rarely did.

"What does it feel like," Nick asked, finally forcing his eyes to meet his father's, "when you're touched by God?"

Fear suddenly leapt into his father's eyes — not quite the reaction Nick had expected. Surprise, maybe. Laughter maybe, but not fear.

"Jeez! Are you telling me you want to become a priest?"

"Hell, no!" said Nick, and then began to wonder whether using the word *hell* in relation to the word *priest* would end up sending him there.

"Listen, Nick," said his father, starting to understand a little bit, "you almost got yourself killed the other day." Nick felt a chill go through him. No one had put that to him so directly before. "And when something like that happens, it shakes things up in your head. It makes you look at things differently." He shrugged, not sure of the truth behind his own words. "I suppose that's good — as long as you don't lose perspective."

Nick nodded, and watched his father as he sadly drifted into memories he didn't want to recall. "Like my friends from Vietnam, Nicky . . . some of them lost perspective."

His father thought for a moment more, then leaned across the table, speaking in a whisper. "Your mother would kill me for saying this to you, Nick, but I've been a police officer for twenty years now, and I can tell you — God doesn't touch people in the city, so stop thinking that way."

Nick nodded again and looked down. Maybe his father was right — but then, twenty years as a police officer could give someone a lousy view of everything. Maybe it was his father who had lost perspective.

"How about in Long Island?" Nick said, with a smirk on his face. His father laughed, breaking the tension.

"Well, in Long Island, everybody's touched," his father said, spinning his finger by his head. They both laughed.

Touched or not touched, it didn't matter to Nick now. He wouldn't talk about it with his father anymore, or his mother. There were no Bible quotes or war stories to help Nick with this. Besides, he had already made his decision without them.

Somewhere in the city there was some other disaster waiting to happen — another golden opportunity — and Nick would be there to save the day. Being a hero again would be easy . . . as long as he believed in his own ability to be one. And next time, he would get to meet the mayor.

The coin flipped up once more.

"Tails," his father said. Nick caught it in his hand. "For the dishes," his father added.

"Sorry, Dad," said Nick with a slim smile on his face. He opened his palm and slapped the coin down on the back of his left hand. "It's heads, I win."

Nick lifted his right hand to reveal the coin. Never once did he look at it.

"Ah," said his father, "you got lucky." He picked up the coin to examine it.

"It's not luck," said Nick, still keeping that slim smile on his face. "It's always heads." Nick gently returned the coin to the laundry saucer.

"It's been heads ever since I left the subway station."

4 · *The Badland Disaster*

The cursed block at Forty-first Street and Ninth Avenue had become a legend in the city. Nothing good ever happened there, and it seemed nothing could save that sad rectangular plot of land, just a few blocks west of all the Broadway theaters New York was so famous for.

The Maximilian Hotel was the first casualty. It stood there for nearly sixty years, and earned the nickname "Hotel of Horrors," because of the many gangland murders that took place there during the twenties and because of the horrific state of decay the hotel had always been in.

Throughout its life, the Hotel of Horrors limped along on the edge of bankruptcy, until, in 1966, the powerful and healthy Bastion hotel chain bought it and tried to restore it. But the powerful and healthy Bastion hotel chain suddenly went out of business a few months later. People just figured it was the curse of the Maximilian Hotel.

The city bought the land, tore down the crumbling hotel, and, with no better ideas, built a park there.

But the soil wasn't quite right. Nothing but crabgrass would grow there, and no one went there, aside from pigeons. Eventually the place became an open-air hospital for any and all diseased pigeons in the city.

Finally the city gave up and put a fence around the block, and there it stood for a year, filled with crabgrass, dead pigeons, and scrawny, stunted trees.

The *New York Post* called it "haunted." The *New York Times* called it "cursed," but most people simply called it "The Badland" — a fitting title — and stayed away.

Martin Lanko called it a challenge, and bought the sorry piece of land in the heart of midtown Manhattan. He planned to take the legend of the Badland and turn it into money, building there "The Badland Hotel" — just one of six Lanko building projects that were growing up around the city like weeds.

Naturally, no one in the city was very surprised when an oil tanker truck crashed into the Badland construction site and exploded.

• • •

Linda heard about the Badland disaster just as she was leaving school, from a friend who had a radio constantly plugged into her ear.

"It's like King Tut's tomb," offered one kid. "Anyone who builds anything there is history!"

Linda didn't believe in things like that.

"Wanna come over with me and watch it burn down?" asked a boy who had been trying to get a date with her for weeks.

"It's not going to burn down," she told him. "There's nothing there to burn." Linda knew the status of most major construction sites in the city, and the Badland Hotel was in its earliest stages. So far, it consisted of only four floors of girders, and concrete — it was nothing but a giant jungle gym.

Still, Linda wasn't going to miss a disaster at the Badland. Although she declined the invitation from the dweeb, when she got in her car, she told the driver to take her right across town to see the damage with her own eyes.

•   •   •

Four intersections had had to be blocked off, and traffic in all directions was at a complete standstill. Linda's driver had to drop her off three blocks away. He warned her, as he always warned her about such things, that perhaps she ought to go home instead. He didn't press the issue, though, because he knew arguing with Linda was a useless endeavor.

Crowds pressed against the barricades to watch the spectacle, as if it were New Year's Eve and they were waiting for the ball to drop. The thing was indeed burning — the truck must have been full of gasoline when it crashed through the sheets of plywood surrounding the construction site and plowed deep into the structure. Smoke billowed between the girders, so thick and so black that the low-rise apartment buildings downwind had to be evacuated.

As Linda slipped through the crowds on Ninth Avenue, she heard rumors of trapped workers, but no one knew for sure.

Fire fighters in full protective gear were dousing the smoking jungle gym with water and foam, but it was like trying to put out a burning oil well. Someone in the crowd suggested that perhaps the accident had ruptured a gas main, and that rumor, too, spread quickly through the crowds.

Linda stood on her toes and looked around until she caught sight of her father standing just inside the police barricade. His long coat and long scarf were too heavy for the warm October day, especially now that there was a fire. He chatted with a policeman, who shook his head a lot and pointed. There wasn't much for either of them to do now. It was all up to the fire fighters. Linda watched her father pace as he viewed the entire scene. It must be miserable for him to not be in control of the show, thought Linda. She had seen him like this before; there had been other accidents — the slab of marble that fell during construction of his Sapphire Pavilion tower, the scaffold that gave way when the sixty-story Lanko Metropole building went up. When you built as many buildings as quickly as her father did, there were bound to be disasters.

But this one seemed worse than the rest.

Even from this distance Linda could tell what her father was thinking. Lanko was wondering whether or not this accident was actually sabotage, and he was slowly convincing himself that it was. In half an hour he would be gripping his ulcer-ridden stomach, wondering how other builders dealt with such disasters.

Across the street, thick smoke poured from between the naked girders. The wind carried it away, but Linda still turned her eyes from it. The smell was not that of a wood fire. It was a harder, dirtier smell, like that of an oil refinery.

Around her the crowd continued to grow, despite all the police efforts to keep people away. Then, as if to aid the police, a gust of wind shifted the smoke in the direction of the crowd. Linda closed her eyes and held her breath until the gust passed.

And then she was hit from behind.

At first she thought someone was trying to grab her purse. She hugged it to her body, twisting instinctively, and saw a boy her age forcing his way through the crowd. He was shoving people with his elbows as if they were cattle. When Linda didn't move fast enough, he grabbed her arm as well, pushing her aside.

Their eyes met only for an instant. Linda was ready to shoot him an angry glance for being so rough, but she could see in his eyes he had no interest in her. He had something else on his mind. In a second he was over the police barricade and racing toward the burning Badland construction site.

What did he think he was doing?

How dare he push her aside like that, and make no apology. What was so important anyway?

Linda couldn't be sure, but she thought she recognized him from somewhere. The curly brown hair. The light eyes. Who did he think he was?

"Nicky, Nicky, wait a second," shouted a voice a few feet behind her. She turned to see a short, stocky teenage boy trying to follow the first boy through the crowds. The second boy stopped at the barricade, afraid to go farther.

"Nicky, whaddaya crazy?" he yelled, but the boy with the curly hair didn't turn back. A cop caught sight of him as he raced across the street, toward the burning site.

"Hey! Hey, you!" he shouted, but he was too late. The wind shifted, and even before he reached the sidewalk the smoke wrapped around the boy like a dark liquid.

For a moment Linda thought the boy might be trying to kill himself, but it didn't seem right. The look on his face was one of determination, not desperation. She pushed her way past a few onlookers to find the boy's friend.

"Hey," she said, "do you know him?"

"I don't know what he's doin'. He's actin' crazy!" The boy took a nervous bite of the pizza crust he was holding, and then threw it to the ground. "I don't know."

"He could die in there!"

The boy shook his head as if to ward off an evil spirit. "No. He ain't gonna die." He took a moment to think about it. "He wouldn't a gone if he didn't know what he was doin'." He looked up at Linda. "Right?"

Linda couldn't answer that. From what she had seen, lots of people did weird things for no reason.

In front of them the updraft from the heat pulled away enough smoke to reveal the naked fire in the heart of the girders. No one could survive that.

"Somebody should do something!" she said, and

pushed against the barricade, grabbing the sleeve of a passing fireman.

"*Do* something?" said the fireman. "What do you think we're doing here, playing hopscotch?"

It was then that the crowd discovered yet another point of interest. Linda heard voices around her whispering back and forth.

"Hey, isn't that the daughter?"

"Whose daughter?"

"You know, Lanko's daughter."

"That's her?"

"Yeah, that's the one, Linda Lanko . . ."

And the news spread faster than "the wave" at a crowded baseball game.

The stocky boy took his eyes away from the fire only once. "You're Lanko's daughter?"

Linda nodded.

The boy turned his eyes back to the fire. "Go tell him to send someone in after my friend."

There was a roar from the crowds. Linda followed the path of pointing hands not to the fire, but to an old apartment building, catty-corner to where she was standing. The boy with the curly hair had just come out of the apartment doorway, half-carrying, half-dragging a man who seemed to be twice his weight, and a thousand years older. The boy standing beside Linda let out a wail of surprised joy. His friend hadn't gone into the fire at all — with the smoke blocking their view, they hadn't seen his real destination, the apartment building. It was one of the low-rises that had been evacuated. Thick smoke was blowing right into the face of that building, and the explosion had blown out most of its windows. It seemed the curly-haired boy had spotted someone in one of those windows that no one else had.

The old man in his arms seemed to be unconscious. The curly-haired boy himself was coughing and gasping. "Way to go!" screamed his friend. He put his fingers in his mouth, and let out an ear-piercing whistle. Then he turned back to Linda, his whole attitude changed.

"So no kiddin', you're Linda Lanko?" said the boy, all smiles now. His smile displayed a row of braces filled with the remnants of his pizza slice. "Never thought I'd meet *you!*"

In the street, paramedics were putting the old man into an ambulance. Linda watched as others argued with the curly-haired boy. He resisted their help, and sort of staggered back toward the barricades, coughing.

"What's his name?" asked Linda.

"Marco!" The stocky boy said, "Marco Mednick." He reached out his hand and shook hers tightly.

"No," she said calmly. "*His* name."

"Oh. He's Nicky Herrera," said Marco Mednick. "Now he's *really* gonna be famous," he mumbled to himself.

"He was famous before?" said Linda.

Out in the street two paramedics had stopped Nicky and finally convinced him to take the oxygen they were offering. In a second they had him on a stretcher, carrying him toward a waiting ambulance. Linda saw all this, but Marco Mednick didn't. Marco Mednick was too busy staring at her. He smiled broadly, but this time with his mouth closed. She could see his tongue working hard behind his lips to clear the pizza debris from his braces before he would show teeth again. Linda sighed. Why was she always surrounded by dweebs?

"So," asked Marco, "you go out on dates?"

"Maybe some other time," she said politely.

"You mean it?" Marco brightened up as if she had said yes.

"No," said Linda sympathetically, "I'm sorry."

Marco looked down. "Yeah. No biggie." He didn't look at her again, and when Linda glanced toward him once more, he was gone.

Across the street the smoke seemed to thin out as the fire fighters delivered high-pressure water into the steel structure. Since it was now clear that the fire was under control and the entirety of New York wasn't about to go up in flames, the crowd began to thin as well.

Hadn't Nicky Herrera rescued someone from the subway last week? Was that why she had recognized him? Was that what Marco meant by "famous"?

By now the ambulances were gone, but a face lingered in Linda's mind — that determined face of Nicky Herrera. She recalled the way he had pushed past her, acting as if she wasn't even there. The sheer rudeness of it annoyed her no end.

Well, at least she could take some satisfaction in knowing that in a city of eight million people she would never have to see that haughty self-righteous face of Nicky Herrera ever again, if she didn't want to.

And if she did, he'd be easy to find.

5 · A Private Invitation

Nick's mother didn't come to the hospital. She called every five minutes until the doctor examined Nick and gave him a clean bill of health, but she wouldn't come to the hospital. "I don't want to see those reporters," she had said. "They ask stupid questions." Other than that, she didn't mention a thing about the rescue. She simply wouldn't deal with it.

"Your mother just gets this way around Salvatore's birthday," his father said — which was ridiculous, because Salvatore's all-important birthday was over a month away — right around Thanksgiving. "Saint Salvatore's Mass," Nick always called it, because on that day the family would, with solemn remembrances, worship the ground Salvatore once walked on. His mother seemed to be starting the weirdness a bit early this year.

Nick's father, on the other hand, did not act like a shut-in. He had come straight over to the hospital in his patrol car, in the middle of his shift. He didn't seem angry, but he didn't seem too terribly pleased either. Maybe he just didn't know what to feel.

"What were you even doing there?" he asked on the way home. It wasn't a reprimand — he genuinely wanted to know. "I mean, that place is halfway across town, Nicky."

"We were nearby, so we figured we'd watch the fire," said Nick in a raspy voice. His lungs still ached from the smoke. It felt as if he had inhaled an entire carton of cigarettes and they were burning in his lungs. Nick rubbed his arm. It hurt as well, because he had ripped the stitches open during the rescue, and they had had to be redone. Now he'd *really* have a scar.

"But what were you even *doing* there?" his father asked again. "School was just letting out when it happened!"

"So?" said Nick with a shrug. "Marco and me ditched school to get some Original Raoul's pizza."

"But why?" asked his father.

"Because there's only one Original Raoul's," said Nick. After all, it wasn't as if Nick had planned to go to the fire. Of course, he did go half a mile out of his way once he heard about it.

His father shook his head. "Nicky, do you always ditch school to get pizza and watch fires?"

"Not usually, no."

His father looked at him for a good long time as they waited at a stoplight, rubbing his forehead as he always did when he couldn't find the words in English or Spanish to say to his sons. As he always had when he used to speak to Salvatore. Nick shifted in his seat and turned away.

"Nicky, you can't go on doin' this stuff," he said. "You're not Superman, eh?" Then he got all mushy. "C'mere." He grabbed the back of Nick's neck and pulled him close, giving Nick a big kiss on the cheek. Salvatore, Nick remembered, never allowed his father to kiss him, and so Nick made a point of allowing it — even in public.

Nick didn't say anything more, because he knew anything he said would not have been what his father wanted to hear. For whatever reason, Nick's life was undoubtedly charmed. He had raced into two ordeals, come away clean both times, and the coin was still coming up heads.

Nick looked at his hands, and marveled at what they had already done. Maybe he wasn't the Man of Steel, but he could be the next best thing — and if he needed to be faster than a speeding bullet, he knew he would be.

●   ●   ●

The *Post* called him "Boy Wonder," the *Daily News* called him "Hero of the Month"; the *Times* said he was "an example for all 'inner city' youth." And *this* time, he met the mayor.

The invitation arrived three days after that.

This was the beginning. Whatever grand machine Nick had thrown himself into, the wheels were set in motion, and things were moving — doors of opportunity that he had never dreamed of breaking down were now opening before him.

It wasn't just that he had met the mayor. It wasn't that the fire department had issued him a certificate of honor at a special ceremony. That stuff was fun and all, but now it was all over, and meeting the mayor was not the big deal he had thought it would be.

It was the invitation that was a big deal.

Nick sat on the fire escape outside his bedroom window, staring at the white, already dog-eared card. The fire escape was his private perch. It was the place where he had determinedly conquered his childhood fear of heights, and now whenever he sat in the small red iron cage, three floors above the sidewalk, he felt at peace and in control. This was his personal throne of conquest, and no one ever went there but Nick.

The invitation had been in three different shirt pockets since he received it, for he wanted to keep it close to him at all times. It was a fine reward for the rescues he had performed, and a reminder of the rescues yet to come.

When he first got it, he wanted to tell the whole school — but he had bragged so much about his rescues, he felt all bragged out, so he kept the invitation to himself. It wasn't that he really wanted to brag about the rescues, but everyone just kept asking and asking, and he had to describe them over and over again. He became an expert storyteller.

"Nobody else saw the old man in the window . . . ," he would say about his fire rescue. That much was true. *"I raced across the barricade at top speed, running towards the old building."* Actually, his bald-treaded old Nikes had hydroplaned on the firehose run-off water, and he fell on his butt before he got to the building.

"The place was starting to burn by then, too."

Not true. The apartment building, while filled with smoke, never actually caught fire.

"The smoke was so thick, you couldn't see an inch in front of your face. . . ."

Actually, he could see pretty well until he got to the third floor. Then the smoke got thick, and his eyes began to burn.

"I musta climbed a hundred, two hundred steps. . . ."

Nope. Three floors; more like thirty-nine.

"I found the old man's door and kicked it in. . . ."

But that didn't work, so he turned the knob. It was unlocked.

"The guy was in his bedroom, on the floor, gasping for air. . . ."

That part was true. Nick found him struggling to get back up to the window, where Nick had first seen him.

"The guy was a cripple. . . ."

Later, Nick learned that the man had broken his hip while hurrying to pack a bag before he evacuated the building. That's when he had crawled to the window and called for help, but his voice could not be heard over the commotion below. The bag he had been packing was still sitting on the bed when Nick arrived.

"We were both about to die from the smoke. . . ."

By now the smoke was getting to Nick. His lungs were burning and his knees felt weak. He started to get scared.

"I hoisted him on my shoulders, carrying him down the stairs."

Well, more like dragging him — the guy was pretty hefty.

"And that's just how it happened!"

His friends loved the story — especially the girls, who fawned all over him. That was pretty good, until all their boyfriends came around and tried to beat the crap out of him.

But that didn't matter now that he had The Invitation.

The fire escape creaked and complained as Nick shifted position, and Nick looked up to see Bozo, his mother's sickly old cat, stretching its thin neck from the top of Nick's bookcase, looking to jump out onto the fire escape with him. Actually the cat's name was Electra, but Sal, Paulie, and Nick all called her Bozo, and Bozo seemed to stick. Nick watched as Bozo halfheartedly leapt onto the brown iron railing with wobbly legs. The cat never looked down because she believed herself to be so surefooted, she would never fall. This was one stupid cat. Its legs slipped, as they always slipped, and the cat fell off, landing on its back in Nick's lap. It flipped over, and looked up at him with its big yellow cat eyes and meowed.

One day, thought Nick, the cat will fall the wrong way and get itself killed. But then, perhaps that would be a more dignified way to go than being put to sleep.

"Why should I put the thing to sleep?" his mother would always say. "She's old, and she's sick. She'll die naturally enough without us helping her along." She was just too attached to the cat to let it go.

In Nick's lap, Bozo immediately began to sniff at the invitation. She knew what was important. Nick sniffed it himself, and swore he could still catch a distant scent of perfume. Probably the expensive stuff, too.

"Hey, Nicky." Marco's voice barged its way into Nick's private little world. Nick looked up and saw, through the slats of the fire escape, Marco poking his head out of his window two floors above.

"What's up?" asked Marco.

"Nothing," answered Nick.

"What's that you're lookin' at?"

Marco was like the old cat; he could sense something interesting a mile away. Fortunately he didn't come down to sniff it, too.

"Nothing," said Nick. "Just a flash card. Trig equacions, you know."

"Oh," said Marco, sounding disappointed. "That's all?"

"That's all."

"'Cause I thought maybe it might be something you might want to tell me about, maybe."

"Not unless you wanna take my test for me," lied Nick.

"Oh," said Marco, sounding disappointed again. "Well, later!" he popped his head back inside, and the window scraped shut.

Marco could be weird sometimes. No, not sometimes, most of the time. But the invitation was none of his business.

Nick closed his eyes and tried to get Marco out of his mind by thinking about the party he would be going to in less than a week.

Across the street he could hear the banging and pounding and scratching and grinding noises of the workers laboring away at a frantic pace to build Lanko Terrace Tower. The shadow of the immense sky crane, fifty feet above the thirtieth floor, swung with a heavy load of steel. It dragged an iron shadow across the front of Nick's building, and across Nick's face. Usually the construction sounds would annoy him, but not anymore. Now they were music. Now they were a powerful reminder of the very card in his hand, and he silently wondered how many people in New York City actually got invited to a Halloween party thrown by Linda Lanko.

•   •   •

"You should take Marco along with you," suggested his mother, as Nick sat alone at the kitchen table for dinner that night. His family never seemed to eat dinner together anymore. "It says you can bring a guest," she added.

Nick stabbed some string beans with his fork. Marco, Marco, Marco! It was getting so five minutes couldn't go by without Nick having to think about Marco.

"Ma," said Nick, "you bring *dates* to parties like this. Not other guys."

"So? You got a date?"

"No."

"So go stag with Marco. You'll meet girls there."

Actually, Nick was planning to go stag — better to risk the chance of spending the night as a wallflower than to bring a date and miss a chance at meeting some high-class girl from a private school. And what if Linda Lanko herself wanted to dance with him? Going without a date would be fine — but how could Nick bring Marco to a party in a Sutton Place penthouse? Marco would use his index finger to eat the dip. He'd scrape the caviar off of the crackers and eat the crackers plain. He'd use those little plastic cocktail toothpicks to pick grunge from his braces. He'd ask all the girls for dates, and, worst of all, he'd tell dead-baby jokes. No. No way. It was out of the question.

"Remember," said his mother, "if it weren't for Marco, Linda Lanko wouldn't know you from a hole in the ground. . . . Besides, Marco's been going around telling everybody Linda Lanko's in love with him — if you don't take him, you'll break his heart."

"He only met her once," said Nick. Marco had told him about his meeting with Linda Lanko, but it was impossible to pick out which parts of Marco's story were true, and which parts he just wished were true. In any case, Nick knew Linda Lanko could not be in love with Marco Mednick.

"Marco," said Nick, "is getting to be more of a liar than Ralphy Sherman." Ralphy Sherman, Nick recalled, once had half their class believing he was dating a Brazilian princess, until she told everyone that she was actually from the Bronx. Ralphy had spent weeks trying to convince everyone that the Bronx was also a city in Brazil.

"If Marco's going to lie like that," decided Nick, "then he has it coming to him." And then he added, "A little bit of humility never hurt anyone."

His mother threw him a holier-than-thou sort of look when she heard the humility line. Humility was something she'd always been on his case about — especially since the rescues.

"What are you going to tell him, hah?" she asked.

"What are we? Siamese twins?" said Nick. "Who says he even has to know about it?"

"He already does," said Paulie, passing by the dinner table, on his way out to some major date. "I told him."

"What?" Was there no privacy in this home? Was Nick's life a public-access TV station? *"What?!!"* screamed Nick.

"I . . . told . . . him," repeated Paulie slowly, as if for a moron. "I hear his mother's already making him a costume."

And with that, Paulie waltzed out of the apartment, whistling happily, like the Angel of Death after a kill.

"Well." His mother sat down at the table and folded her arms. "I guess a little humility never hurt anyone," she said triumphantly. Nick hated it when she said things triumphantly.

"So, big shot, what do you say now?" she said.

What did he say? He was cornered; what could he say?

"How do you make a dead baby float?" said Nick, with a sigh.

His mother shook her head. "You're disgusting," she said, and she piled another slab of meat loaf onto his plate.

•   •   •

It was cold out on the fire escape after dinner, but Nick didn't feel like going back inside to get a jacket.

After dinner Nick had called Marco and invited him to the party. Needless to say, Marco had been thrilled to accept.

"See how easy that was," his mother had said.

Bozo stood on the windowsill, sniffing the air. This time she didn't try to jump to the railing, she just sauntered over to him.

Why couldn't friends be more like cats? he thought. All a cat ever wanted from anyone was to be fed. It didn't need to be told everything about your life. It didn't demand to be invited to every single party *you* were invited to. You didn't really have to worry about hurting a cat's feelings. Nick wished, for once, he didn't have to be such a "good friend."

Across the street the construction work had stopped for the evening. The tower was silent, the arm of the sky crane waiting patiently for the morning.

A wind blew through the skeleton tower, almost whistling. Soon it would be finished. Soon his whole block would probably be torn down to make room for towers like it. All it took was money, and the power to wield a sky crane.

It was bound to happen someday ... but Nick would be out by then, and Marco wouldn't stop him.

Somehow this hero business was going to get him out.

In spite of Marco, he would make use of the party, by meeting important people, doing all the right things, gaining everyone's admiration with the stories of his rescues. This party was a test, and he was determined to do better than a D+.

This rescue stuff, Nick knew, didn't just "happen." It was put before him for a reason, and maybe part of that reason would be made clear to him at Linda Lanko's party.

In his arms, the cat began to shiver, its thin fur not quite protecting it from the wind.

"What do you think?" he asked Bozo, and the cat responded with a halfhearted meow, and a shiver. Well, whatever it was all leading to, he would certainly find out soon enough.

Nick slowly brought his hand to the old cat's back, and gently, gently stroked her fur until she stopped shivering and fell asleep.

6 · Michelangelo, Van Gogh, and the Lindbergh Baby

Nick's costume did not work out as well as he would have liked. The invitation said, "Come as a work by your favorite artist," but Nick had never spent much time thinking about who his favorite artist was. Paulie, who was taking an art history class at NYU, suggested Nick go as one of Andrew Wyeth's newly discovered paintings, which sounded fine to Nick, until he found out that that Andrew Wyeth's newly discovered paintings were all of a woman named Helga.

Paulie apologized for the slight oversight, and then suggested Nick go as Michelangelo's statue of David, since Michelangelo's David had curly hair like Nick. This too sounded like a good idea, until several days later, when Nick tried to come up with a costume. It was then that Nick discovered Michelangelo's David was naked.

Well, there was only so far Nick was willing to go for the sake of art.

Nick refused to ask Paulie for further advice, and instead went shopping to try and find something he thought Michelangelo's David might have worn, if David could have shopped at Bloomingdale's. He also bought a slingshot, since David used one to kill Goliath.

The costume he ended up with was no costume at all, but by then it was too late to do anything about it.

Marco, on the other hand, went as a very convincing Self-Portrait of Vincent Van Gogh.

•   •   •

"So, whaddaya think?" asked Marco, as they stood together on the corner of Second Avenue and Ninety-fifth, waiting for a cab to take them to the party. Nick had to admit that Marco's costume was brilliant. His mother had painstakingly covered a shirt and pair of pants with heavy brush strokes, so it looked as though Van Gogh had painted the clothes himself. Marco wore a red wig, and a red goatee beard. His costume was infinitely better than Nick's.

Marco held a small box up to Nick. "Here," he said. "Take a look."

Nick took the small white box from Marco. Something inside made a dull thud-thud-thud as he shook it.

"What is this?"

"Open it up," said Marco, all smiles.

Nick glanced at Marco, then slowly lifted the lid of the small box. He was faced with a rubber ear, on a bed of bloody cotton balls. Marco began to laugh hysterically. He turned his head to reveal a piece of duct tape covering his right ear.

"Isn't this great?" cackled Marco. "Isn't this perfect? They'll love this at the party!"

Nick gave him back his box, and put his hand in the air to hail a taxi. "You ain't wrapped too tight," said Nick. A taxi weaved across three lanes on the one-way avenue, and stopped in front of them. Nick told the driver the address.

"They say Van Gogh cut off his ear and sent it to his girlfriend," said Marco, as they stepped into the cab. "You know what I think?" he said. "I think maybe I oughta give it to Linda Lanko."

"You do," Nick warned, and "I'll cut off the other one."

Again Marco cackled wildly, and as the taxi sped off, Nick began to rub his forehead, like his father.

· · ·

The city was full of taxis carrying ghouls and witches, clowns, and ballerinas. While very few kids were trick-or-treating, adults were taking Halloween very seriously. Everyone seemed to be throwing a Halloween party. Everyone had a halfway decent costume.

"Hey, Nicky," asked Marco. "What's the matter, huh? Don't you like my costume?"

Nick sighed. "Your costume's great, Marco," he said. "Anyway, it's a lot better than mine."

"Yeah, it is, isn't it?" said Marco proudly, as he held his rubber ear up to his face and peeped through the ear-hole. "So ... who are you supposed to be, anyway?"

"Michelangelo's David."

Nick looked up to catch the cab driver's eyes in the rearview mirror. The driver was laughing at Nick.

"Oh," said Marco, as he leaned back in his seat. "I didn't know they wore ties back then."

That was the last straw.

•   •   •

Mona Lisa opened the bleached wooden door of the one and only penthouse atop the one and only Lanko Sutton Chateau — and Mona was faced with Nick Herrera's bare chest, which she stared at speechlessly.

Now, as Nick stood there at Linda Lanko's threshold, he concluded that taking off his shirt in the elevator was perhaps the most humiliating of all possible moves. And, even though he hadn't remembered what she looked like, he instinctively knew that this Mona Lisa was, in fact, Linda Lanko in a brown wig.

He smiled weakly, and his lips quivered in immeasurable embarrassment. "Hi," he said.

She was cool about it, although her eyes kept darting back to Nick's unbelievably bare chest.

"Hi, Miss Lanko," said Marco. "I almost didn't reco'nize ya!" He reached out and shook her hand as if he were trying to take her arm off. "Remember me? I'm Marco Mednick — I asked you for a date and you said no, remember?"

This she handled coolly as well. The corners of her mouth turned up in the slightest smile, like the Mona Lisa. She turned to Nick and his bare chest.

"And you must be Nicky Herrera."

"Nick," he corrected. It was bad enough his parents and Marco still called him Nicky — after all, he wasn't in kindergarten anymore. Nick looked around. There were at least thirty guests already filling up the immense two-story living room, and everyone was in costume. One girl had one shoulder higher than another, and an eye in the middle of her forehead. She was a Picasso. One guy had a blue face, yellow lips, and green hair. He was an Andy Warhol. And everyone, *everyone* had on some sort of shirt.

Nick's cheeks were already flushing in embarrassment, and he imagined the flush moving down his neck and across his painfully bare pectoral muscles, stretching down toward his ridiculously bare belly button.

"Well," said Linda, now keeping her eyes firmly, almost hypnotically, locked on Nick's eyes. "I can tell who Marco is — but who are you supposed to be?"

Nick showed her the slingshot, and said weakly, with a crackle in his voice. "I'm Michelangelo's David . . . after he could afford to buy some pants."

By now his toes must have been flushing as well.

She gave him that Mona Lisa smile. "But that's cheating," she said, and Nick began to wonder if he would be asked to remove the rest of his clothes to make his costume complete. Why did he have to come to this party?

Just then a blond boy with vinyl clocks melting over his shoulders and stapled to the rest of his clothes approached the doorway.

"What's this?" he said, his upper lip curling in an Elvislike sneer.

"Kyle," said Linda, "this is Nick Herrera. You remember, he's the one who rescued all those people." Actually, the tally was only up to two, but Nick didn't feel like correcting her. "He's Michelangelo's David."

Nick held out his hand to shake, but Kyle wasn't shaking. "So," said Nick, "what are you supposed to be?"

"I'm Salvador Dali, moron," said Kyle, and Nick prayed Marco wouldn't ask who Salvador Dali-Moron was.

"I'm Van Gogh," said Marco. "Wanna see my ear?"

"I think Nick's costume is fabulous." said Linda. "Don't you think he makes an excellent David, Kyle?"

Kyle snarled with Elvis lips again. "I think it's stupid," he said, as a melting vinyl clock slipped from his shoulder onto the ground. "That's not even the right kind of slingshot."

"Hey, Kyle," someone yelled across the room. "What time is it?" A bunch of kids broke out laughing.

"Aw, shut up," said Kyle. He picked up his melting clock and walked away.

Nick turned to see that Marco had left as well, having spotted the buffet table. Nick and Linda were alone.

"I think your costume is the most original and the most daring one here," she said. "And that's what Halloween is all about, isn't it? Being daring?"

Nick smiled, almost feeling comfortable. He didn't speak just yet, for fear that his voice would crack again. She must have thought he was an idiot.

"Come on," she said. "There are some people here I'd like you to meet."

"Should I put my shirt on?" he asked.

"Of course not," she answered. "Not until *everyone* gets a chance to see your costume."

Nick could feel his face going from embarrass-ment-red to seasick-green . . . and oddly enough, this seemed to please Linda Lanko no end.

•   •   •

It didn't take long for Nick to learn a great deal about Linda Lanko. It wasn't that she told him any-thing — in fact, she never told anybody anything about herself. Just by observing, Nick was able to piece her together.

First of all, she seemed to own just about every-thing in the world. Second, she seemed to know just about everyone in the world. Third, she did anything in the world she wanted to, whenever she wanted to do it, and her father didn't seem to care. At one point, Nick glanced around at the few adult chaper-ons and servants at the party, and asked Linda if her father was there.

"My father," Linda told him, "is away, buying some property in Chicago." She brushed back her Mona Lisa hair. "Isn't that convenient? Lanko's a very con-venient man. Never around when you don't need him."

Nick also came to understand why he had been invited to the party. He, in his own little way, had become semifamous — and Linda Lanko loved noth-ing more than to surround herself with famous peo-ple, even if she had never met them before. In fact, as Nick slowly discovered, very few of the people at the party were actually Linda's friends. Most of them were just people she had heard about. She had invited them and they had come, because everybody knew that anybody who was anybody under the age of eighteen in New York was nobody unless they attended one of Linda Lanko's parties. The list of people she introduced Nick to during the course of the evening read like a page from *Who's Who*.

Nick met Max "I've-been-on-the-cover-of-*Time*-magazine-twice" Barbett, the sixteen-year-old Olympic gold medal diver, who was so full of himself his head could explode at any minute. He was dressed as a medieval painting of Jesus Christ. Nick's mother would not have been pleased.

"I'm the only diver ever to get perfect scores from all the judges in all my events," bragged Max. He also contended that other divers were afraid to compete against him.

As they walked away, Linda whispered to Nick, "Don't you just love it? He's *sooo* conceited!"

Next came Yvette Valbon, the French tennis player. Only fifteen, she had taken fourth place at Wimbledon, and was now dressed as one of Toulouse-Lautrec's can-can girls. "I took the Concorde in from Paris this morning," she told Nick in a heavy French accent, and Nick wondered whether she had other business in New York, or had she just flown in for Linda's party.

Linda introduced Nick to a black girl in a white dress, as "Francine Delaney, who knows five languages, and is the chairperson of the United Nations Special Youth Committee on International Disarmament."

Nick held out his hand to shake, only to discover that Francine, indeed, had no arms.

"I'm Venus de Milo — the statue," she said, "and it doesn't have any arms. Actually, I do have arms, but they're behind my back."

"Doesn't that hurt?" asked Nick.

"Not anymore," she said.

Across the room, Nick heard Marco's voice delivering a punch line: ". . . a scoop of ice cream, some root beer, and a scoop of dead baby." Nick was glad he was somewhere very far away.

•   •   •

The list of V.I.P.'s was unending, and Nick got to meet perhaps only a third of the people there: the teenage boy with his own television show, the Chinese violin virtuoso, a senator's daughter. Nick was beyond starstruck, and greeted them all in a barechested daze while Linda weaved her way back and forth through the crowd, like a circus plate spinner, trying to keep an ear or a voice in every conversation.

One more thing Nick noticed about Linda was that she needed to know what everybody was doing at every moment.

Perhaps it was just his imagination, but it seemed to him that as Linda flitted around, introducing people, and mingling with her guests, she spent a bit more time with him than with anyone else. Maybe it was just because he didn't have a date. In any case, Kyle noticed it as well, and seemed about ready to pop some springs in his melting clocks. Linda and Kyle exchanged secret nasty looks all evening, but avoided each other like the plague. They had to be going out together, concluded Nick. Two people didn't hate each other *that* much unless they were going out.

"Best party of my life," said Marco, as he swept past Nick, on the way back to the buffet table. "I'm tellin' everybody I'm the President's nephew." Sometime later, some debutante found Marco's ear sitting on a Ritz cracker and nearly had a coronary.

• • •

A twelve- or thirteen-year-old boy dressed as Beethoven's Fifth Symphony had been standing in the corner for most of the evening. Being the youngest person at the party, he must have felt more out of place than Nick and his bare chest, so Linda dragged Nick away from a rather mind-boggling conversation with a fourteen-year-old astrophysicist to save this lonely guest.

The Beethoven boy seemed quite pleased that someone was coming over to speak with him. "Bobby O'Donnell, I'd like you to meet Nick Herrera. Nick rescues people."

They shook hands. "Bobby," said Linda proudly, as if showing off one of her favorite collectibles, "is the world's youngest pilot."

"Oh, right, I heard about you," said Nick. "You're the Lindbergh Baby!" The press had been calling Bobby the "Lindbergh Baby" ever since he first recreated Lindbergh's transatlantic flight at the age of ten. Most recently he had been in the news for being the youngest pilot ever to fly a plane twice around the world.

"So, what are you going to do next?" asked Nick.

Bobby responded as if he had it all planned out in his mind already. "I'm going to be the youngest civilian ever to fly in the space shuttle," he said.

"You think you can do it?"

"I don't know," he said, then thought for a moment. "But what else is there to do after you've flown twice around the world?"

Armless Francine overheard their conversation, and sort of stumbled into it.

"Bobby said he'd take me up in his plane," said Francine.

"Well," said Bobby, blushing, "I said I'd ask my dad. . . ." He scratched his nose, and dislodged a musical note from his cheek.

"Oh! Will you take me in your plane?" asked Linda.

Bobby hesitated, but he just couldn't turn down his host.

"Sure," he said. "I guess."

"Great!" said Linda. She thought for a moment, then glanced at her watch. "It's nine o'clock. What time should we leave?"

Everyone laughed, except for Linda, and Nick could tell by that Mona Lisa smile on her face that she was not kidding. This girl was dead serious.

"Hey," said Linda, "it's Halloween, isn't it? So we should do something really daring! What's more daring than taking a late-night flight with the Lindbergh Baby?"

Bobby's eyes began to dart back and forth like a rabbit in a small cage. "But . . . but . . ."

"But, you can't just leave your party," said Francine, jumping to Bobby's aid.

"So, we'll go after the party." Linda's excitement was growing, and Nick could feel it fueling his own. There was something about this girl that made her different from any other girl he had known — and it wasn't just her money. "It'll be great," she said. "Just the four of us."

"I . . . I'm not allowed to fly," said Bobby, "unless there's another pilot on board."

"Well, that's silly!" said Linda, dismissing it entirely. "If you can fly, you can fly. Can you fly?"

"Yeah . . ."

"Then there's no problem."

By now Max of Nazareth had heard their conversation and had slipped on in.

"Just imagine it," said Linda. "Soaring high above the city, on Halloween night. Just the *five* of us." She pulled Max into their little circle. "Where's your plane?"

Nick watched the conversation in amazement. Linda Lanko could squeeze Perrier out of a stone! She was good. She was *really* good. In one minute, she had everything planned out. They would take a cab into Jersey, be dropped off at a Holiday Inn, then sneak across the street to Teterboro Airport to take their flight. The whole affair would take less than three hours.

"But it's impossible," pleaded Bobby. "My dad's picking me up at eleven!"

"No he's not," said Nick, out of the blue. "Not if you're at a slumber party."

Everyone's head snapped around to see him, as if Nick had just appeared out of nowhere.

"Huh?" said Bobby.

Nick put on a deep voice that sounded fairly convincing. "Hello, Mr. O'Donnell?" said Nick. "Yes, this is Martin Lanko. . . . My daughter has decided to throw an all-night video party, and since it is Saturday, we didn't think you'd mind if . . ."

Linda grabbed his arm, accidentally squeezing his stitches. Nick grimaced. "That's great!" she said.

By now Mai-lin, the Chinese concert violinist, who spoke barely any English, and had come dressed as a

Norman Rockwell painting, had wandered toward the conversation. She took one look at Bobby, lifted her violin, and tried to play him, but since he wasn't really Beethoven's Fifth Symphony, it didn't sound like anything. She stopped playing and stood there, trying to figure out what they were talking about. Linda grabbed Mai-lin's arm, and pulled her into their little circle. "It'll be great," said Linda. "Just the *six* of us." Linda smiled at Mai-lin, and Mai-lin smiled back, thrilled to be included in whatever was going on.

"But . . . but . . ."

Bobby seemed just on the verge now . . . all it would take was one tiny little push to get him to agree — just a little bit of incentive . . . and Nick, having once been thirteen years old himself, knew exactly what was needed.

"I guess he's just afraid," said Nick.

Bobby's jaw dropped open.

"It's OK," said Nick, in an understanding voice. "If I were a pilot, I'd probably be afraid to fly without my father too."

"I *am not* afraid," said Bobby, as if this accusation was a slap in the face.

"Well, sure you are," said Linda, picking up on Nick's cue. "But that's OK, really."

"I am not!" he said again. Now he was getting angry.

"Sometimes it's good for children to be afraid," said Nick.

"*I am not!*" protested Bobby. "I can fly alone if I want to — whenever I want to!"

Linda smiled that Mona Lisa smile again. "Sure, you can, Bobby," she said as if speaking to a very small child. Nick could see in Bobby's eyes the moment he made his decision.

"Where's your phone?" he said, pushing his way past Linda. "*I'll* tell my father about the slumber party."

Bobby stormed off, never realizing that he had just been played like Mai-lin's violin. He marched across the room, right past Marco, who was sitting with, of all people, Kyle. Marco had given up on his jokes, and Kyle had given up on Linda, so they both sat together in front of the television, content to watch the stars of the World Wrestling Federation pound each other to bloody pulps. They made an interesting couple; Vincent Van Gogh and Salvador Dali.

Linda looked over and saw them too.

"What about *them*?" asked Nick.

"Well," said Linda, with a flick of her brown Mona Lisa hair, "we can't take *everyone* with us."

7 · Confessions at 15,000 Feet

What couldn't be accomplished with a great deal of nerve, simply couldn't be accomplished. This was Linda Lanko's philosophy. Nerve had gotten her father where he was today, and Linda had no reason to believe it would work any differently for her. So far nerve had gotten her everything money could not.

Security was always lax at small airports — especially at this time of night. People simply didn't expect a fifteen-year-old girl to march into tiny Teterboro Airport at one in the morning with five of her "closest friends," and take an unauthorized sightseeing flight. She knew that since no one expected them to be there they would have no problem in getting away with their little Halloween escapade.

While Max and Francine still had their doubts, they made the calls home, and didn't even need Nick to perform the voice of Martin Lanko. Mai-lin, who was thrilled to do anything Linda asked, brought along her violin for some live entertainment. Linda felt certain this was going to be a great deal of fun. It would be an event none of them would ever forget, and if there was nothing else she could share with them, she would show them how to have fun on a dark Halloween night. It was the least she could do.

As they approached the plane, sitting quietly, parked beside dozens of other small planes, Bobby began to mumble to himself. "My father," he said, determined to prove to them he wasn't afraid, but still looking a bit ill, "is going to kill me when he finds out about this."

"He doesn't have to find out," said Nick, taking the words right out of Linda's mouth. It pleased her that they thought alike. Linda smiled at Nick and decided that he was much better looking than Michelangelo's David. Perhaps not better looking than Kyle, but infinitely more interesting — and in a way, infinitely more dangerous. He was almost as wonderfully dangerous as a midnight flight with a thirteen-year-old pilot.

Linda figured she'd kiss Nick before the night was over, just to rattle his brain a little.

No one said much as the plane taxied toward the runway, and since the airport was officially closed, no one from the tower bothered them. In a moment, Bobby was accelerating to take off.

"You realize," said Max, "that we could all die up there."

"More people die in car accidents than in airplanes," Bobby said with confidence and a professionalism far beyond his thirteen years. It was amazing to watch him, so much more at home behind the control panel than he had been at Linda's party.

"Besides," said Linda, "we can't die. We're all too important." She tried to imagine how the headline would read if they actually crashed. She wondered which of the six of them would get top billing.

The single-engine Cessna picked up speed. Its nose rose into the air.

"It's my first time flying," Nick blurted out, and then looked away, as if embarrassed. Linda took his hand and held it, careful not to bump his stitches as she had so clumsily done before. It felt good to hold someone's hand because she wanted to, rather than because she was simply supposed to.

The rear wheels left the ground, the craft took off into the dark night, and once they were safely in the air, everyone — even Bobby — let out a much-needed sigh of relief.

Now they were all there, cramped into this tight cabin — Mona Lisa, David, Jesus, Beethoven, Venus, and Norman Rockwell. Linda hadn't really known these people before her party — but now they would be bound together by this secret flight.

That's how friends were made.

For a while everyone silently watched the rows or streetlights twinkling below — everyone but Nick. Mai-lin pulled out her violin, tuned it, and began to serenade them with glorious strains of Mozart at ten thousand feet. The music filled the tiny cabin, and although it didn't drown out the sound of the engine, it made everyone forget about it.

The plane ascended toward the belly of the clouds, and as the cottony billows began to scrape across the top of the plane, the tiny craft shook and vibrated with turbulence. Everyone looked to Bobby to see how he would react.

"Relax," said Bobby, with calm professionalism. "Clouds are easy."

In a moment their view vanished and was replaced by the thick gray fog. The plane rattled and shook but then, a few moments later, the clouds thinned, and the craft stabilized. They were riding above soft moonlit cloud cover, so much brighter than below that their eyes had to adjust to the blue light.

This was another world up here, and everyone's troubles seemed to have been filtered out by the cloud layer. Bobby didn't talk about his father and Max didn't seem quite as conceited as they rode just above the ceiling of the world.

"Hey, Lindbergh Baby," asked Max. "Which way is the city?"

"That way," said Bobby, pointing to a glowing patch of cloud cover. "And I wish you wouldn't call me that. My name's Bobby."

"Sorry," said Max. "It's just that I forgot your name."

"You know," said Francine, "we really don't even know each other at all."

"Then let's get to know each other," said Linda, leaning in a bit closer to Nick. "Let's tell something about ourselves that nobody else knows."

"Truth or Dare?" asked Francine.

"No," said Linda. "Just truth."

The air in the plane got a bit thinner. Linda's ears

popped. No one spoke. Truth was not an easy thing.

"Who goes first?" she asked.

No one volunteered.

"OK," said Linda, "I'll go first . . . I . . . I . . ." She bit her lip, thinking. "I'm adopted," she said. "I was adopted by Martin and Elsie Lanko when I was six weeks old. Lucky me. Next?"

It took a few moments, but Nick was the next to speak. Somehow Linda knew he would be.

"I used to be really afraid of heights," he offered. "So I sort of forced myself out into high places, and made myself look down, until it didn't bother me anymore," he said, and then cleared his throat. "But sometimes it still does."

"Like when?" asked Francine.

"Like now," said Nick, with a nervous chuckle.

Linda nodded her approval of his confession. "Next?" she said.

"Well," said Francine, "I once choked on a jawbreaker and almost died. Is that good enough?" Everyone turned to Bobby.

"Sometimes I get airsick when I fly," said Bobby. "It's really gross."

And the game had begun. Around the cabin it went, to Linda's delight. Everyone played except for Mai-lin, who was more than happy to play her violin passionately and watch everyone else. By round four, they were practically jumping over each other to get their confessions in.

"I'm not very good in math."

"I had an out-of-body experience once."

"I flew before I had my flying license."

"My dad once bribed a diving judge."

"I never really liked my ex-boyfriend."

"I once beat up a teacher."

"I stole a pair of jeans last month."

"I've got a crush on Bobby!"

Francine covered her face after she let that one fly, and everyone laughed, even Bobby, who, on the ground, would probably have turned beet red.

It wasn't until the sixth round that things began to get a little creepy. By now Mai-lin was in the slow, brooding movement of some deep, dark requiem. The sound of the engine had been tuned out of everyone's mind. The plane seemed to hang above the heavy blue clouds in silence. It was Max's turn. He took his time. He rubbed his eyes, and looked out at the clouds, then turned toward everyone in the cabin. He made eye contact with Linda, but broke it off and looked at his knuckles, as he began to crack them.

"I hate diving," said Max. "I hate it."

No one said anything for a while.

"Why do you do it?" asked Bobby, for the first time turning away from the controls.

Max shrugged, and popped his thumb knuckle. "Why do you fly?" asked Max. "Do you like it?"

"Sometimes."

"All the time?"

"Not all the time," said Bobby.

"Then how come you do it?"

"Because I have to, that's all," said Bobby. "I just *have* to." There was a long silence, filled with nothing but a legato B-flat from the violin. "What would I do if I didn't fly?" asked Bobby, more to himself than anyone else.

Max took his time. "I used to get a real rush from diving . . . but lately I get up on the platform, and all I feel are pains in my chest. . . . and I get to thinking about my cousin who keeled over at twenty-two when his heart called it quits. Twenty-two!"

Max began to rub his chest hard, as if he wanted to dig his fingertips right through his sternum. "And when I'm up there, I get afraid each time I dive that . . ." but he couldn't finish. He stopped rubbing his chest and looked away from everyone. "Anyway, I don't like it. That's all."

"I always thought being an Olympic star would be a good thing," said Nick.

Max looked up at Nick with anger and resentment in his eyes. "Who are you to talk? What do you know about it?" said Max. "All you've ever done is rescue a couple of people. Big deal. You don't have to train every day of your life, whether you feel good or bad. You don't *have* to rescue people, do you?"

The violin changed keys. B-flat to A, major to minor.

"Yeah, I do," said Nick, in a voice that was barely a whisper. Linda watched Nick closely. He was going to say something, Linda could tell. Something big. Something important. and for an instant, she almost didn't want to hear it, but she had to, because it was Nick's turn to tell a truth. "I have to rescue people," he said. "I think maybe I'm supposed to. . . . Anyway, I don't think I can stop." He didn't say anything more. Instead he pulled a coin from his pocket. A quarter.

"I showed this to my dad," said Nick, "but he didn't really believe me."

Bobby set the controls on automatic, and turned to

face the rest of them. Mai-lin stopped playing. In that blue moonlight, just above the clouds, at 2:15 in the morning, Linda swore she could feel something funny going on . . . as if her mind were slipping away. As if the plane were flying into the Bermuda Triangle.

She watched Nick's thumb as he flipped the coin.

"Call it," he said to Linda.

"Heads," she said. The coin landed, and he slapped it to the back of his hand, then revealed it. It was heads.

"So?" said Max.

Nick flipped it again. "Call it!" he said to Francine.

"Tails," said Francine. The coin came up heads.

"Big deal," said Max. Nick flipped it again.

"Call it," said Nick, to anyone who wanted to.

"Tails," said Mai-lin, in a thick accent.

The coin came up heads.

"Call it!"

"Tails!" said Bobby.

The coin came up heads.

Max reached into his own pocket, and substituted a dime for Nick's quarter.

"Now try it," said Max, figuring he knew the trick. The coin flew, over and over again.

"Tails!" called out Mai-lin. The coin showed heads.

"Tails!" called out Francine. The coin showed heads.

"Tails!" called out Bobby. The coin showed heads.

A gust of turbulence rattled the plane and threw it to the left. Bobby returned to the controls, but only for a moment.

Nick flipped the coin again, and slapped it to the back of his hand.

"You call it, Max."

"I don't want to."

"Call it!"

"I said I don't want to!"

Max glanced around the cabin, and stared at the back of Nick's hand, which hid the dime. He sighed. "Heads?" he said.

Nick lifted his hand to show Roosevelt's unmistakable profile. Heads.

"At first I thought it was kind of funny," said Nick, "then I thought it was kind of weird. Now I don't know what to think about it. It's like all of a sudden nothing I do goes wrong."

"So," said Max, his voice just a little bit shaky. "What does *that* have to do with rescues? What does that *prove?*"

Nick shrugged. "It's like I got this talent for being lucky. That's how I figure it . . . and if I got a talent, I should use it, right?"

"There's no such thing as a talent for luck," said Linda. "If it's luck, then it can't be talent, can it?"

Nick rubbed the coin between his thumb and forefinger. "I don't know," he said. "You tell me."

The plane rattled violently with turbulence again, and Bobby returned to the controls, but this time the turbulence didn't stop. They had gone in a huge circle, but now the clouds seemed heavier, and darker. The wind rattled the plane like a loose wind chime.

"Let's go down," said Max, "before we crash into a jetliner," and everyone agreed.

They all relaxed a bit when Nick gave Max back his coin. Even Linda. She now knew there was more to this Nick than met the eye. He was more dangerous than she had imagined, and she didn't know whether she was afraid of it . . . or if she liked it.

Bobby held the controls but didn't do anything. He had been confident through the whole flight, but it looked now as if his confidence had just run out. And it seemed he was going to tell them a truth.

"I guess it's my turn to confess something," said Bobby, with a shaky voice. "There's something I never told you . . . ," he said. His face was pale, warning of the airsickness he had admitted to earlier. "It's not that I'm afraid or anything . . ." He looked at Linda, and she decided right then and there never to play this game again. "It's just that I've never landed a plane at night before." Bobby's face turned even more white.

". . . I've never even flown at night."

•   •   •

The starry night sky vanished, covered by a gray void, as the plane began a rocky descent through the clouds.

"This was a bad idea," said Max. He was the only one who said anything. They were beneath the clouds now, and the shimmering streetlights of suburban New Jersey scrutinized them from more than a mile below.

"I've seen my father do it," said Bobby. There was sweat on his face, even though the cockpit was getting uncomfortably cold. "Landing's the easiest part of flying . . . really." It sounded like he was trying to convince himself. His hands shook and Francine held an airsickness bag out to him.

"I'm *not* afraid," he said. "I really think I can do it."

"You *think* you can do it?" said Max. "He *thinks* he can do it?! Oh great! We're gonna be dog food in about five minutes!"

"Shut up, Max," said Linda. "You're scaring him."

Bobby suddenly let go of the controls, grabbed the bag from Francine, and was sick. The plane careened to the right. Bobby, still holding the bag, could only control the plane with one hand. "Usually when I get sick," he said, between gasps of air, "my dad takes over for me."

By now Francine had had enough, and she moved to the back to sit next to Mai-lin. Chinese was not one of Francine's five languages, but the two girls communicated perfectly the same language of fear. Mai-lin halfheartedly picked up her violin and tried to play some cheerful Vivaldi.

"Stop it!" yelled Max, and the music died.

Linda wasn't going to let this get to her. She knew how to fight fear; she would simply get angry at it, and the fear would go away. *People don't die as a result of airsickness,* she tried to tell herself. *That would be ridiculous. Besides, this was my idea — I wanted to be daring, and I can't let this ruin an otherwise perfect evening.*

Bobby was violently sick again, and his hands slipped away from the controls. Every few seconds he tried to look up, but then his head would fall back down between his legs. The ground kept looming closer.

"Let Nick do it." The words blurted out of Linda's mouth before she even knew why she said them.

Nick looked at her, as if woken up from a dream. "Huh?"

"If you're so certain it's your purpose in life to rescue people, then rescue us." She spoke calmly, trying to hide anything that resembled panic, and she watched Nick closely. How would he react? Did he seriously believe in his own luck, or was he just another fake, like so many of the people she knew?

"Are you nuts?" said Max.

Nick looked at his hands — as if staring at them gave him some sort of strength. Then he looked Linda right in the eye and through her, as he had done when he raced to rescue that man from the fire. He brushed past her to take control of the plane.

"He's serious!" cried Max. "He's friggin' serious!"

But it was as if everyone else in the plane was caught up in the spell Nick had woven the moment he began flipping that awful coin.

"Max, shut up," said Francine from the back.

"Yeah," added Mai-lin.

Bobby was too sick to say anything at all. He just slipped weakly over into the passenger seat when Nick pushed him aside. He tried to protest, but could barely lift his face out of the airsickness bag.

Max seemed ready to blow up from explosive decompression. "You people are nuts! All of you!" he said. "There won't be enough of us *left* to be dog food!"

No one even dignified him with a response, so he went searching through the cabin, mumbling about a parachute.

Below, the streetlights seemed brighter, and were moving by much more quickly. The altimeter read 2,000 feet.

"Pull up," Bobby mumbled. "You're going down too fast."

Nick pulled back on the steering column. Once Nick lifted the nose, he seemed to have it under control. He regarded the control panel with the same concentration Bobby had. Linda watched Nick's eyes and could see him absorbing the information as if he had picked up a book written in a foreign language and instantaneously knew how to read it. He must be brilliant, she thought.

Max now sat next to Linda in crash position. "I don't want to die in an air disaster," he moaned. "I really don't."

Way ahead of them was an island of darkness, and on the island were the blue landing lights of the small runway.

Linda had never seen anyone with such intense concentration. Her father would sit for hours studying real estate deals without saying a word, but that was nothing compared to how Nick took in the instrument panel, and the runway far ahead.

As the plane neared the runway, the turbulence stopped. They soared through the air as if riding on the crest of an invisible wave. More than that — it seemed to glide in the soft grasp of an unseen hand, and that feeling terrified Linda more than the violent turbulence had.

This was a feeling she couldn't understand, and always refused to think about — even now, a hundred feet from the ground, within an inch of her life. If Nick safely landed that plane, she would be forced to face the possibility that Nick's luck was not luck at all, but a gift — and if it were a gift, then where did it come from? If Nick became the hero now, it raised impossible questions she didn't dare answer. She suddenly knew she could not let Nick land that plane.

"Bobby, take the controls," she said, in not much more than a whisper.

"Huh?"

"Bobby, take the controls!" she screamed. "Just do it! Just do it! Just do it!"

Around them, the reality of their situation snapped back into place violently. My God! What were they doing? They were letting a guy who had never even been on a plane try to land one! Max was right; they were all out of their minds!

So shocking was Linda's panic that it broke Nick's concentration and made Bobby forget how uncontrollably airsick he had been. Nick slid over and Bobby took control of the plane. The runway loomed closer and closer. The island of darkness surrounded them. The blue runway lights began to fall off on either side of the plane.

The plane bounced hard. A wing dipped. It bounced again, more softly this time, and the third time it touched gently, staying on the ground and slowing to taxiing velocity.

Bobby let out a chestful of air, "Told you it was easy," he said, wiping the sweat from his brow. "*Now* who's afraid?"

Nick sat in silence, looking down, until the plane pulled into its parking spot. Bobby shut down the engine, and then went out to put blocks beneath the wheels. "My father's going to kill me," he mumbled.

Now that they were once again on solid ground, the spell was completely broken. The spell that made them believe that the coin business could be anything more than just a trick of the odds.

There was a race to get out of the cabin, but Max managed to be the first one out. "It'll be my pleasure," said Max, "if I never see *any* of you *ever* again for the *rest* of my life." He left, followed by Francine and Mai-lin. Apparently they weren't about to suffer any more time together, even to finish off their slumber-party charade.

Nick and Linda climbed out together, the cold night hitting them. Linda took a deep breath and purged herself of the foul-smelling air that had filled the tiny cabin. A sense of dread seemed to follow her as she stepped out onto the airport tarmac, and that was not so easily left behind.

• • •

"I could have done it," said Nick, as they stepped through the hole in the airport fence. "I could have." Nick's eyes were wet and just a little bit wild.

"You really believe that?" said Linda.

Linda watched him. He looked different now, but then everything seemed to look and feel different at three in the morning. Yes, Nick was definitely more dangerous than Kyle, and more interesting — but also dark, and unknowable. She felt just the tiniest bit frightened of him, and she had never felt frightened of anyone ever before. Not her father, not her teachers, not anyone.

The place was wrong — the timing was not right, but still Linda thought about giving Nick that calculated kiss she had planned — not because she had planned to, but because she wanted to. She had never *really* wanted to kiss a boy before — not like this. Kissing Kyle was never a big deal. She kissed Kyle when he came over to visit; she kissed him when he left. She kissed him to annoy Dina Mitchell, and she kissed him at the movies, when the movie was dull. She had never wanted to kiss him the way she wanted to kiss Nick right now. It was as if Nick had some sort of power over her now, and she thought how quickly her own life could go from heads to tails — how quickly she could lose control of a situation. She had invited Nick because she thought he might be a mildly amusing boyfriend. But now something else was going on.

Linda prided herself on living by her impulses and was annoyed at her own hesitation. If she wanted to kiss Nick, well, then, she should kiss him. And so she did. She took his hand just before they crossed the road, and when he turned to her she firmly planted one right on his lips, determined not to break away until he did. But he didn't break away, and it rattled Linda enough for her to pull back first. Although they had kissed for perhaps only five seconds, it felt like half a minute.

That he was as rattled as she was made her feel the tiniest bit better.

Nick stuttered a bit before he spoke.

"I ain't never kissed someone rich before," Nick said, letting his English slip into shades of Marco. "Haven't," he corrected himself. "You don't *really* like me *that* much, do you? You're just kissing me, right?"

"No," said Linda, "I really do. I really do like you Nicky ... Nick," she said, correcting herself. She hated herself for openly admitting this to Nick. She should have just smiled her Mona Lisa smile, like she always did. "Never let people know how you feel," Lanko had taught her. "It gives them the upper hand." *Stupid!* She should have just smiled.

But if Nick had the upper hand, he didn't use it. He just slipped his hand around her waist gently —

almost meekly — and they walked toward the hotel, where they'd call for a taxi back to the city.

• • •

During the cab ride, one thing kept playing over and over in Linda's mind.

Nick was going to get himself killed with his rescues. Somehow or another he had gotten this idea into his head, and it was going to kill him, plain and simple.

Linda's was a world of steel towers, and concrete streets — it didn't have room for things she couldn't explain. There could be no magic, only mathematics. No miracles, only coincidences — and although there were many things that could be accomplished with a great deal of nerve, there were also a great many things that simply couldn't be accomplished at all. Period.

As she sat in the cab, her knee touching Nick's, she began to feel angry and confused. How dare he make her feel so out of control? How dare he come into her life, only to get himself killed? She felt she wanted to kiss him again, and hold him, and protect him from subway trains and fires and every other danger. How dare he make her feel like that?

"Linda," said Nick, when they were halfway back to the city. "I really could have done it. I really could have landed that plane."

"I know," she answered, almost believing it — and it frightened her.

8 · Bench of Morons

Six o'clock on a Tuesday night. A week after the fateful flight, and two weeks before Nick would have to suffer through Salvatore's birthday. The evening was brisk, but not too cold. Not yet, anyway. Although it was already dark, there were plenty of respectable-looking people around Nick and Marco, as they sat on a Central Park bench at the north end of the reservoir.

Sitting in Central Park was just something Nick decided he had to do.

Marco had insisted on joining him after Nick had shown Marco his coin trick. His showing Marco that trick was looking more and more like a major mistake.

"You know what I think?" said Marco. "I think you had this weird mental ability since you were born, and never knew it. I bet you can do all sorts of things like bend spoons with your mind and stuff. Ever try bending spoons with your mind?"

"No," said Nick.

"Well, you should try it," said Marco. "Ralphy Sherman says his aunt bends entire sets of silverware each time she sneezes in the kitchen."

"Yeah," said Nick. "Ralphy Sherman also says he bought a nuclear warhead by mail order."

Marco thought about it for a moment. "It's probably an exaggeration, huh?"

Nick chuckled, and continued to wade through the stack of schoolwork he had brought to the park with him. The street lamp above gave him just enough light to work. Marco glanced at his work, then back up at Nick.

"If I could bend spoons like you, Linda Lanko would be going out with *me* instead."

"I can't bend spoons!" said Nick.

"Yeah," said Marco. "But *she* doesn't know that." Marco turned to his textbook angrily and flipped a page.

Well, Marco certainly did have reason to be jealous, didn't he? Linda Lanko had kissed Nick, and that was more than ninety-nine point nine percent of the guys in the city could say — and Nick figured that Linda Lanko was not the sort of girl who kissed lightly. Once she kissed you, it probably meant things were pretty much official. In the week since that fateful kiss, they had seen a lot of each other: once on an official date, and twice just hanging out after school. This was only the beginning.

"Don't forget, I saw her first," mumbled Marco, dropping his textbook to the concrete, and picking up one of Nick's Steroid Avenger comic books. To

Marco, Linda was a mountain upon which he had staked his claim, and Nick had come along to throw him off a cliff.

Nick turned up his worn leather collar to the chilling wind. He wondered what Linda would do if she knew he was sitting on a bench in a dangerous part of Central Park after dark. Would she be angry, would she think him brave, or would she care at all? It was hard for Nick to figure out how she really felt about him, and sometimes Nick wondered if her liking him was some part of a joke, or maybe even a dare by some of her rich friends. After all, how could a girl like her possibly like him, especially after their horrifically formal and humiliating first date?

"This is my father's date," Linda had explained that night, as they sat in the fancy restaurant, "not mine." She wore a pink gown and Nick wore a gray sport coat that he had worn at one wedding and two funerals. It was too short in the sleeves and made Nick feel like a gorilla for the entire evening. He probably would have felt more comfortable going as Michelangelo's David again.

Linda had to order for him, since he couldn't read French. Their first course was a pâté, which Linda described as "chopped liver with an attitude." Nick, who despised liver with a passion deep and true, ate it for Linda's sake, but came seriously close to tossing his cookies all over his fine imported china. He had scraped more appetizing pâté specimens off the sole of his shoe.

The soup was cold and had fish in it, and the main course was a bird with its head still on. It looked up off the plate with unhappy oven-roasted eyes.

"This isn't pigeon, is it?" Nick asked in all

seriousness, and Linda laughed and laughed, applauding his sense of humor.

The meal was officially paid for by Martin Lanko. They were officially chauffeured by Martin Lanko's limousine, and for a grand finale, when the date was officially over, Martin Lanko drove Nick home in his sporty Jaguar, so he could give Nick his official man-to-man talk.

"I care a great deal about my daughter," Lanko had said. "So I hope you don't mind if I act a little concerned."

He then went on to grill Nick, as if he were interviewing him for a top-security job. Lanko made a point of exploring Nick's background and yet didn't seem troubled when Nick discussed his less-than-extravagant life. He wasn't even bothered when he saw Nick's old building across the street from his own luxurious tower. In fact, he made a point of telling Nick, "I grew up a lot like you," whatever that meant. Where Nick came from and where Nick was ultimately going, however, didn't seem to matter as much as did Nick's intentions toward Lanko's daughter.

"I care a great deal about Linda," he reminded Nick again, as he stepped out of the Jag that night. "She's a fragile girl. I don't want to see her hurt."

Nick knew this was something he didn't have to worry about, for he had no intention of hurting Linda — and besides, as far as being fragile went, Linda Lanko was about as emotionally fragile as a bulletproof vest.

It was Nick who was feeling just a bit vulnerable, and as Martin Lanko drove away that night it occurred to him what a huge expedition dating Linda Lanko was turning out to be — how many people it involved and how much effort it required just to impress her. In a sense it *was* like climbing a mountain. It seemed like one misplaced foot could send him plummeting back down to where he started. Eventually he figured he'd be able to take a moment to sort out how deep his feelings for Linda really went, but right now he was simply working too hard to think about it.

In any case, he guessed that Linda would be pretty impressed if Nick pulled off tonight's little Central Park maneuver. And he'd be pretty impressed himself.

• • •

At 7:00 the reservoir track was still packed with joggers. Nick knew that joggers ran around the perimeter of the reservoir through all hours of the night, and they were occasionally attacked. It couldn't be much longer until someone was mugged. People drown in reservoirs, too. It was a good place to wait.

"My dad," Marco said, "says anyone who walks through Central Park alone late at night deserves to get mugged as a punishment for stupidity."

• • •

By 9:00 Nick's patience for schoolwork had worn out, and comic books filled the void. The joggers had thinned out, but there were still plenty of them — maybe twenty or thirty — running around the track. Still nothing.

A cold front had moved in, and the temperature

had dropped. When the boys spoke, they spoke in little puffs of steam.

"Does anyone know we're here?" asked Marco, and Nick shook his head. "Somebody should know in case we're murdered by a pack of satanic psychos and our hearts are ripped out."

• • •

By 10:30, even the comic books felt like homework, and Nick's nose was beginning to run from the cold. The joggers were few and far between now. Only the fearless ones remained, one or two passing by each minute. Otherwise the north end of the reservoir was a desolate, lonely, and vulnerable place. But nothing happened. And then something occurred to Marco that apparently had never occurred to him before.

"Why are we here?" asked Marco.

"You know why," said Nick. "We're waiting for rescue opportunities."

"No, I mean why are we *here*? Why not somewhere else? Where it's warm, at least."

"Because I had this dream a few nights ago," mumbled Nick.

"What was it about?"

"What do you think? It was about the reservoir."

"Yeah, but what happened in it?"

"I don't remember. I just remember it was about the reservoir."

"Well, if you don't remember," said Marco, "how do you know something happened? Maybe it was one of those boring dreams where you sit on a bench for four hours like a total moron and nothing ever happens. Maybe you dreamt that? You think so?"

Nick sighed, and decided to call it an evening. "Let's get the hell out of here." Served him right for trusting a dream.

No one bothered them as they made their way out of Central Park. No muggers, no gangs, no human-heart-eating-satanic-psychos. Nothing. It really pissed Nick off.

"I thought Central Park was supposed to be dangerous," he said.

It was then that Marco submitted these pearls of wisdom. "You know what I think? I think maybe this hero stuff isn't something you can go looking for. Maybe it's something that has to come to you, or it doesn't work."

Nick picked up his pace, heading toward the traffic of Fifth Avenue, which ran along the eastern edge of the park.

"I know what I'm doing," said Nick, dismissing Marco's words. But the words lingered longer than most of Marco's generally stupid comments usually did.

"This coin thing," said Marco, as they stepped out onto Fifth Avenue; "it's gotta mean more than just rescues."

"What? Are we talking about bending spoons again?" scoffed Nick.

"No. I don't know, but something. Maybe even something big." Marco shook his head. "It's just that miracles don't happen for no good reason," Marco said.

"The coin thing's not a miracle," said Nick. "It's just a *thing*. A *thing* that *happens*."

Marco held his shoulders low. "Well, it doesn't happen to me," he said. Marco stood there looking awkward and confused. "What's it feel like," asked Marco, as serious as could be, "to know you can't lose?"

In front of them the light changed, but neither of them made a move to cross the street.

"I don't think about it," said Nick.

"If it was me," said Marco, "I'd always think about it. I wouldn't be able to stop thinking about it. Even if I *did* have Linda Lanko on my mind."

The Don't Walk sign began to blink and the light changed back to red. A bus rumbled by, splashing mud to the sidewalk as it drove through a pothole the size of a small lake. Nick switched his now-spotted books from one hand to the other.

Marco was quiet for a moment, and in the tense silence, Nick fought the urge to pull out a coin, and flip it — for what if he did and it unmiraculously landed on tails, like a coin ought to, half the time? What if his good fortune had all been spent, and he had performed his last rescue? No. There were just some things that Nick didn't dare think about, and that was something Marco simply could not understand.

"I'm coming back here tomorrow," said Nick, making his decision. "And the next night, and the next." Marco just stared at him, his mouth dropped slightly open. "And I'll keep coming back until something happens," said Nick. "Are you with me?"

It took a moment, but at last Marco nodded. Nick smiled and turned to cross the street. There would be another rescue. Maybe not right away, but soon — and most definitely before Thanksgiving and "Saint Salvatore's" damnable Mass. This year his family would have something to give thanks for.

Nick crossed against the light, with Marco following in his wake, and, although both lanes of traffic blared their horns and came to screeching halts, no one dared to run over Nicholas Herrera.

9 · The Grid

Martin Lanko had built the Sapphire Flame at the base of his seventy-story Sapphire Pavilion, under the pretense that the city needed more under-twenty-one clubs, and "wasn't it a crime that so few places were built with teenagers in mind?"

The truth, however, was much more transparent to Linda than the royal-blue glass of her father's eight-sided edifice. He built the Sapphire Flame in order to keep a tight reign on all of Linda's dates, plain and simple.

The bouncers at the club worked for her father, the DJ's worked for her father, even the alcohol-free bartenders at the alcohol-free bar worked for her father. In the two years since it opened, the club had been a smashing success — and why not? Lanko had spared no expense in making it enticing, so that Linda would want to go nowhere else on a Friday or Saturday evening.

Linda, of course, hated the Sapphire Flame with every bit of her soul. And yet her father still managed to win, because all of Linda's friends always wanted to go there. So Linda found herself there more often than not.

This is where Linda took Nick for their second "official" date. From the very outset, Linda had no intention of going in. She planned to wait for the chauffeur to drive off, and then the two of them would hop in a cab and slip away to anyplace else in the city that wasn't owned by her father.

But Nick, who probably dreamed of being admitted into the Sapphire Flame, seemed so starstruck as they drove up, Linda didn't have the heart to shuttle him away without at least one dance.

"Is there really a waterfall around the dance floor?" asked Nick. "Is it true that the bar is surrounded by fire and the ground is always covered by a thick blue fog?"

Linda smiled in embarrassment for this amusement park attraction her father had built. "Yes," she said. "Makes it hard to find your keys if you drop them."

As they entered through the spaceship airlock that was the front entrance, Nick gawked at the flames, the fog, the waterfall, and the live neon-blue flamingos prancing about in the pond. Linda could only roll her eyeballs. "Welcome to Lankoville," she said.

The music was loud, even when the dance was slow, and Linda wondered how people ever talked to each other in places such as this. This was definitely not where she wanted to be with Nick.

The "Flame" was fine for Kyle — Kyle never had much to say anyway, and she knew everything she needed to know about him before they ever went out. But the boy she danced with now was an enigma. After knowing Nick for two weeks, what did she really know about him? She knew he had enough money to live, but not a whole lot more. She knew he was half-Italian and half–Puerto Rican and that the kids used to call him *Fajita-Pizza,* so he used to get into lots of fights. She knew he had a brother who was dead, whom Nick refused to talk about, and another whom Nick wasn't really close to.

And all of this she had to drag out of him, as if Nick was ashamed of it. How could she tell him that she was ashamed of the things she had, the same way Nick was ashamed of the things he *didn't?*

There seemed to be no way to tell him, and so every once in a while Linda could sense a deep lonely distance between them. It came and went in seconds, lingering just long enough to bother her. It came even now, as they danced close.

Half an hour later, Linda dragged Nick, mango daiquiri in hand, out of the mindless noise of the Sapphire Flame. Once in the street, she hailed a taxi, out of view from their chauffeur.

"Where are we going?" Nick asked.

"You'll see," she answered.

• • •

Carnegie Hall was everything her father's buildings were not. A solid brick structure with no marble facade, or tinted glass windows. It was simple and unpretentious, which was how Linda was coming to like things.

After buying two overstuffed sandwiches at the deli across the street, Linda led Nick around the back of the huge hall, where music could be heard, tinny and distant, like a small radio in someone's pocket.

"Manhattan's full of little tricks," said Linda, sliding her finger down the edge of the stage door, and grasping it near a dent in the metal frame, "and I know all of them."

Linda gave a good tug, and the tinny, distant music exploded into a rousing brass band, filling the alley with rich melody, as the door swung wide.

"Hurry," said Linda, "before anyone sees us."

Once inside, she got her bearings quickly. She told Nick she knew the wings of the Carnegie Hall stage well, but in truth this was only the second time she had done this. And Kyle had chickened out even before they reached the grid.

Onstage the big band played swing music to a nostalgic audience. The stage manager and stagehands didn't have much to do during the number, so they watched from the wings while, in the shadows behind them, Linda led Nick to the rear corner of the stage, to a steel spiral staircase, so steep and so narrow it might as well have been a twisted ladder.

Nick hesitated, looking up at the helix that seemed to disappear through the roof. This was where Kyle had chickened out. Linda hoped Nick was not going to disappoint her as well.

He peered up at the staircase. "It's like the stairs in the Statute of Liberty," he said.

"You've climbed those stairs, haven't you?" asked Linda.

"Yeah," said Nick weakly. "Lots of times."

The applause rose for the musical number as Nick and Linda climbed up and up.

• • •

High above the wooden floor of the Carnegie Hall stage was a steel lattice — a false roof that hung fifty feet above the musicians' heads, suspended like clouds above the city. Here, high above the hanging stage lights, the staircase ended.

"This is the grid," said Linda. "Most theaters have them. It lets the workers get up here and repair things." To Linda the grid was the ultimate location of nondetectability. It seemed one of the few places in the city out of her father's domain.

"Shall we dine?" she said. She hung her coat on the railing, then stepped off the catwalk and onto the grid. Her footfall on the steel cable reverberated deeply, like a guitar string, but the music below was so loud the sound could not be heard.

Linda looked down. From way down below, the grid resembled a piece of graph paper, but up close the dimensions of the graph were much clearer. The mesh of the grid was woven so as to leave foot-wide squares that one could actually fall through if one were exceedingly clumsy, or just plain stupid. Linda took her other foot off the catwalk, planting it firmly on the grid.

"OK, your turn," said Linda.

Nick was not too pleased, but did as Linda asked. He put one foot onto the grid, and then the other. Soon they were cakewalking themselves toward the middle, where they finally sat, their legs dangling through the mesh.

It was as Linda began to eat her sandwich that she noticed Nick trying to spread some mustard with a plastic knife. His hand shook so badly that a big glob of mustard flew off and dropped past the lights, splattering on the white tuxedo shoulder of the first trombone.

The musician probably thought a jaundiced bird had taken up residence on the grid.

Nick looked up at Linda and down at his shaking hands. "I lied," he said. "I've never climbed up in the Statue of Liberty."

Nick took a big bite of his sandwich, filling his mouth so he would have an excuse not to say anything more. There were beads of sweat on his forehead, but then Linda was sweating as well. It seemed all the heat of Carnegie Hall rose up to the grid and stayed there with nowhere else to go.

She took his hand, which was cold, and held it tightly. There was something very charming about Nick when he was ill at ease, and she wondered how she liked Nick better — timorous and vulnerable as he was now, or invincibly self-confident as he had been in the airplane. She found it curious and delightful that such opposite sets of feelings could exist in one boy. Yet it also made her feel uneasy, and she wondered how such opposite feelings as delight and distress could exist in *her*.

As she looked at him, she caught just a hint of discoloration around his right eye. She had seen it earlier, but had thought that it was just the swimming shadows of the Sapphire Flame. The longer she regarded it, the more certain she was that it was a black eye.

"How did you get that?" Linda asked.

Nick smiled slightly, relaxing a bit, as if he'd been waiting for her to ask. "Some guy was mugged in Central Park the other night," said Nick. "I sort of jumped in and saved him."

Linda was shocked, but somehow she was not surprised.

"It was really something," said Nick. "I wish you would have been there to see it. . . . I take on this mugger single-handed, right? And I beat him up, until he just runs away — then this guy — the guy who was mugged, I mean — he's so scared, he nearly has a coronary, right there on the ground. So I . . . so I . . ." And then Nick just clammed up.

"So you what?" Linda prompted.

"Nothing," said Nick. He shifted uncomfortably, looked down, remembered where he was, and his hands tightened their grip on the cables beneath him. "It's just . . . wouldn't it have been something if this guy up and croaks of a heart attack, right after I save him?" Nick chuckled nervously, but Linda didn't find anything funny about it.

"Anyway," said Nick, "the mugger popped me in the eye before he ran away, and that's how I got the black eye."

"It's a good thing he wasn't armed," said Linda.

"He was," said Nick, with a hint of pride. "A switch-blade. But I kicked it out of his hand."

Linda simply stared at him.

The hot air and echoing music made Linda's head begin to spin. It seemed that, along with her father, the rest of the world had slipped through the grid, like water through a sieve. Maybe it was the very reason why places like this were the best places to talk, and tell truths. Dangerous and desolate places. Exotic, and absurd.

Yes, Linda had to admit, she created plenty of danger for herself, but Linda's danger was quite different from Nick's. Her danger was calculatedly rational, while Nick's was wild and untamed. He could have been killed at any time, during any rescue. That he received a mere black eye in his most recent excursion did not change that fact.

"There's something I need to know," she finally asked him as she shifted her seating on the grid. "And I need to know the truth."

Nick put down his paper plate, balancing it on the intersection of two heavy cables. "Yeah?"

Sitting on the grid, Linda dared to challenge him on something she would not even hint at with her feet planted on the ground. "I want to know . . . what you believe . . . ," said Linda, for lack of a better way of putting it.

Nick shrugged. "I'm Catholic," he said.

"No, that's not what I mean. . . ." Beneath her she could feel the uncomfortable cables of the grid cutting off the circulation to her legs. Even in the heat, her toes were as cold as Nick's hands. "I mean, what do you believe about *yourself*?"

Nick threw her a puzzled gaze.

"I mean . . . ," she said. "When we were in that airplane . . . and I gave you the controls . . . you really thought you could land that plane, didn't you? You *believed* you could."

"Yeah," he said. "Didn't you?"

Linda refused to think about that. "So do you believe you could land a plane *now*?"

"I don't know," said Nick. "I'm not in a plane now. Put me in a plane, and then I'll tell you."

Linda curled her toes in her tight shoes. She couldn't get them warm. "But . . . what do you think about while you're doing these things? Do you think about getting on the news?"

Nick shrugged again, and it made her angry. "I don't think," he said. "I just do it. It's like a sneeze or something; it just happens."

"Aren't you afraid?"

"Not while I'm doing it," said Nick, matter-of-factly.

"But *why?*" said Linda. "Why aren't you afraid! You should be, Nick! If you're afraid up *here*, you should be afraid out *there!*" She spoke full-voice now, but the loud brass far below drowned out her words to all but Nick. "Do you think you've got special powers? Do you think you've been chosen to save the entire city of New York, and nothing can hurt you?"

Nick took a long time to answer. "If I believed that," Nick finally said, "then I'd be crazy, wouldn't I?"

Linda didn't answer. Far below, the number ended and the applause rose, then fell. In the silence between songs Nick spoke again.

"I don't know which is scarier," said Nick. "Being crazy, or not being crazy."

Linda didn't know the answer to that one either.

Nick's plate slipped off the beam and wedged in a pulley ten feet below.

"Maybe I'm just plain stupid," Nick said.

"No," she said. "No, you're not." And she leaned over and kissed him until she could no longer feel her toes.

10 · Hell's Waiting Room

Bozo the cat frisked across the floor in Nick's room as if she had overdosed on caffeine. She hopped around like a young kitten as she batted a superball. She hadn't had so much energy in years.

"She's probably gonna die today," said Paulie, peeking his head into the room, straightening his tie. "They say you get a burst of energy right before you die."

Their mother walked by, reached up, and whacked Paulie on the side of his head.

"Whaddaya talking about?" she said. "She's happy because she knows today is Salvatore's birthday."

This year, "Saint Salvatore's Mass" fell on the Saturday after Thanksgiving, and, as it had been for the past few years, the holiday feast that used to be attended by a dozen relatives had dwindled down to just the four of them plus Marco. It was like a private wake.

"I'm glad someone's happy about it," Nick mumbled to himself, but his mother caught it and threw him a nuclear kind of gaze. She was always a full powder keg around Salvatore's birthday. Recently she had been leaving Bibles around the house for Nick, opened up to pages on humility and the sin of Pride. Whenever his mother spoke in Bibles, it meant her powder keg was about ready to explode. They hadn't been on the best of terms since Marco accidentally shot his mouth off in front of her about the Central Park rescue. Fortunately, Marco's slip didn't paint the whole picture. She didn't know that it had happened at ten at night. She didn't know that it was their third night waiting in the park. And she didn't know about what happened after the mugger ran away.

What she heard was enough to get Nick a heavy reprimanding that was perhaps only a six on the Richter scale. Nick was still waiting for the big one.

Bozo danced happily around the floor, not caring in the least about the tension that filled their home like static electricity.

Well, it will all be over soon, thought Nick, and everyone, including his mom, would lighten up. Just a few more hours, and the "visit" with Salvatore would be behind him.

Nick thought it was a sick sort of affair. He hated going; he hated thinking about it. He wished no one would ever talk or think about Salvatore again. But he didn't dare say that to anyone, so he dressed up, like everyone else, and went along quietly.

This year Linda had insisted on coming, too. He had made it a point not to invite Linda to their somber little Thanksgiving dinner — which she obviously resented, so she invited herself to Saint Salvatore's Mass.

She hadn't met Nick's parents yet, and had decreed that today would be the perfect time. "I want them to know I'm a sensitive, compassionate person and I can deal with things like this," she had said. "They'll respect me for it."

That was the reason she gave, but Nick knew the truth. She simply loved watching other people's weirdnesses, and Salvatore's birthday was always a fine opportunity to observe weirdness.

● ● ●

Linda arrived at 10:00 — right on time, as she always did, dressed to the teeth, as she always was, in the height of fashion and taste, not enough to look obnoxious, but just enough to look very, very rich. Her fur coat was probably worth all their furniture put together.

"Don't say anything dumb," he had told his family earlier. "Just treat her like a *normal* person." But he should have known that he was wishing for the impossible.

While Nick's dad went out to get the car, Mrs. Herrera entertained Linda.

"You should tell your hotshot father," she said, as she came out of the kitchen with a plate full of cream-filled cannolis and other Italian pastries left over from Thanksgiving, "that he stole our view." She pointed to the half-finished tower across the street.

Linda took a moment to respond. "Oh. Well, I'm sure he didn't do it intentionally. . . ."

"She's joking," Nick whispered in Linda's ear, and Linda immediately changed her reaction to a laugh.

"Maybe," said Paulie, "your dad could give us a nice new apartment there, since you and Nicky are going out."

Linda laughed.

"He's *not* joking," Nick whispered in Linda's ear. So Linda just smiled politely at Paulie, and Nick nervously shoved a cannoli into his mouth, nearly swallowing it whole.

Where most people would be afraid to even mention the name, Linda was bold and daring. "How often do you 'visit' Salvatore?" she asked.

Bozo raced across the room, took one look at Linda, and vanished at light speed into the bedroom. It didn't look like she was going to die today.

"We all go on his birthday," said Nick's mom. "I also go on Christmas and Easter. I used to go more, but . . ." She smiled and shrugged. "Have a cannoli." Linda took one and ate it daintily. Nick went for his third.

"Well," said Linda, "I think it's a wonderfully caring thing to do." And then she said, "Sometimes I go to the cemetery too, to visit my grandparents."

Mrs. Herrera looked up at her in surprise, and then her eyes shifted over to Nick.

Nick took a deep breath, picked up a napkin, and wiped pastry flakes from his mouth. "We're not going to a cemetery," he said.

"But . . ." Linda, for the first time since he had known her, seemed speechless, and Nick wished he had told her the whole truth before she'd come. "But I thought . . . I mean, didn't you tell me that . . .

Didn't you tell me Salvatore was . . . dead?"

Nick took his time swallowing his cannoli.

"He is," said Nick.

• • •

The dark tower of King's County Hospital stood only fourteen stories high, but still, it loomed over the lower buildings of Brooklyn like the spire of a hellish cathedral. The tower was cold and unfeeling — and no matter how many medical wonders actually took place within the walls of the immense brick fortress, to Nick it would always be overshadowed by that tower. It could be seen from almost anywhere in Brooklyn.

His father used to tell them that, when he was a boy, he could hear the wails and cries of the mental patients locked away in that tower. But he didn't talk about that anymore.

Salvatore hadn't begun his "sentence" at King's County Hospital.

He had started in the gothic white brick towers of New York Hospital, and when it became clear that he wasn't planning on dying, his parents transferred him to English Hollow Convalescent Home — the nicest place they could find, and more than they could afford, since Sal was no longer covered by Dad's insurance. The money that was supposed to go toward a house in Long Island all went to keep Sal in a pretty room with a view that he couldn't even see.

"He's been in King's County for two years," Nick explained to Linda, as they drove across the Brooklyn Bridge. "We needed money to send Paulie through NYU since it's so expensive, and Uncle Steve, who's got some big job at King's County, said he'd fudge the books and put Sal in a good room for only eight hundred a month."

"Why couldn't you just bring him home?" Linda asked, and Nick pretended he hadn't heard the question. Everyone else shifted uncomfortably in their seats.

"Does he like it there, at least?" she asked, not yet fully grasping the situation.

"I don't think he cares much," answered Nick.

•   •   •

They arrived just before noon, and made their way down the endless corridors. The place stank like any hospital, of antiseptic, alcohol, and old floor wax. The fluorescents above them flickered and buzzed, painting everyone in sickly shades of pale olive.

The room was 529. Not in the tower. Thank God it wasn't in the tower.

This was the part Nick hated the most. All their heels clicking on the black-and-white tile floor, as they made their way toward the doorway, counting the odd numbers on the right side of the hall. 505, 507, 509.

Linda wasn't so far off; it was like a cemetery, only without the ivy. It was like walking down thin little graveyard streets, past rows of identical stones, until they suddenly recognized where they were. That's all any of Salvatore's places had ever been. Graveyards without ivy.

513 . . . 515 . . . 517 . . .

What was it Salvatore always used to say? "'Life's a bitch and then you die.'"

"Hmm?" Said Linda. By now they were several paces behind the others.

"That was Sal's favorite expression." *Only it wasn't true*, thought Nick. *Sometimes you don't die.*

"Were you and Salvatore very close before . . . the 'accident'?"

Nick felt himself grow angry. Not at the suggestion that they might have been close, but at the idea that it had been an accident. It was time people started calling a spade a spade.

"My brother was shot trying to rob a grocery store at gunpoint. Shot by the shopkeeper himself." It was no accident. He remembered the night vividly. He knew Sal had been shot, but no one told him the whole truth for over a day. Nick had to hear it from Marco, who, even at the age of ten, was the neighborhood's master of gossip.

Some sort of cruel justice put his own father's patrol car on call that night and made his the second car on the scene. An even crueler justice left Sal like this, so they couldn't just bury him. Perhaps, thought Nick, this was what they meant by Purgatory. This was Hell's waiting room.

519 . . . 521 . . . 523 . . .

Linda chose not to deal with the ugly truth. "Then I guess you don't remember him much," she said.

Remember? Nick remembered Salvatore, all right. Salvatore dressed well, was very hip, and very, very funny. He was also incredibly cruel and very selfish. He would constantly beat up on Paulie and even on Nick, and always got whatever he wanted from them because he was bigger, and meaner.

Nick was too young to know back then that Sal was

just a kid with an attitude, and lots of nerve. Not enough nerve to get him anywhere, but enough to get his brains blown out. Nick recalled spending much of his childhood swinging between absolute admiration for and intense fear of Salvatore. But now he knew exactly how to feel. It was easy. He simply hated him.

"No" was his answer to Linda. "I don't remember him at all."

525 . . . 527 . . . and at last 529.

Dad went in first. The door was slightly ajar, so he knocked. For a split second Nick nearly panicked, thinking he heard Salvatore answering in a gravelly, atrophied voice, but it was only the creak of the door.

Inside, the room was immaculate and smelled strongly of pine. Uncle Steven, knowing they were coming, had arranged the whole show. He had even sent up a few baskets of flowers to adorn the windowsill.

In the bed, Salvatore sat in serene and never-ending meditation. His hair and nails were neatly trimmed, his face freshly shaven. He wore what Nick recognized as last year's birthday present from Mom — a Bloomingdale's knit sweater. The nurses had put it on him at Uncle Steven's request. There was a watch on his arm, too. The only props missing were a cap, sunglasses, and a glass of iced tea with a paper umbrella in it.

The whole thing was obscene. It was like a sick joke, one of Marco's jokes. But, with the exception of Nick and Linda, no one else seemed to notice.

"Hi, Sal," said Mrs. Herrera, tears already beginning to gush from her eyes. She kissed him on the forehead. "Happy birthday," she said.

One by one they said their hello's, Dad trying to sound different from Mom, Paulie trying to sound different from Dad. Nick waited for last. He could have gone on waiting.

"Nicky," his father said gently, "come on over and say something to your brother."

This is all part of the joke, thought Nick.

Nick let go of Linda's hand — as bold as she was, she was not going to get any closer to Salvatore.

How do you make a dead baby float?

As Nick got closer, he could see that Salvatore was remarkably pale, his cheeks were sunken in, and his lips parted slightly as he breathed. And yet it seemed to Nick that his eyes could open at any moment and a big broad smile would appear on his face. He wouldn't move, he *couldn't* move — he was in an irreversible coma — but still, Nick used to have nightmares about it. Salvatore would reach up and grab him by the throat, and paralyze him, pulling Nick down into the bed, then he would run away, leaving Nick the one unable to move, unable to think, and barely able to breathe, forever and ever in the hospital bed. If Salvatore could, he would do it, Nick was certain of that.

Nick looked at Sal's hand resting on the bed. The muscle in his forearm was a tiny little knot. His fingers were curled almost into fists. They weren't like Nick's hands. They never had been. They had never done anything good for anybody.

"Hi, Sal," said Nick, refusing to touch him. "Good to see you."

Nick knew he'd have a nightmare waiting for him that night.

"I didn't know it was like this," Linda told Nick, as

they stood together near the door, while everyone else complained about how hot the room was, how cold the bed was, and how the nurses didn't come in often enough.

"I'm really sorry about this," whispered Nick. "I wish we could just get the hell out of here right now."

Nick's mother, seeing them mumbling to each other, decided to bridge the gap across the room. "So, what do you think?" she said to Linda. "Salvatore is a handsome boy, even still," she said. "Just like Nicky."

Linda smiled uncomfortably, and glanced over at Sal. "Yes," she said, politely. "He does look a lot like you, Nick."

"Mama," said Nick, "don't start this now. Please."

"Start what? I just called you handsome; what's wrong with that?"

"You know what I mean." He said it a bit louder. "Just shut up about it, OK?"

"Nicky," said his father, rubbing his forehead, "not today, eh?"

His mother shook her head. "Some mouth you got on you," she said. Then she turned to Linda. "His brother had a temper like that, too," she said. "Always screaming at me, Mama this, Mama that. Everything was always a fight with that one."

Nick felt his breath becoming short, his hands tightening into little fists like Salvatore's. "Can we leave now?" he asked. "We've seen him, we've wished him a happy birthday, now let's leave."

"Don't be so impatient," said his mother. "You're always so impatient."

"Yeah," said Nick, "I know. Just like Salvatore."

His father began to scratch his hair, which was one step beyond rubbing his forehead. His mother shot

Nick her nuclear gaze, almost daring Nick to ignite her keg.

"Go on," said Nick. "Why don't you just go on and tell all the other ways I'm like Salvatore, Ma? Why don't you?"

"Nick," commanded his father. "Not now!"

"No," said his mother. "He asked me a question, I'm gonna answer it," she said, staring Nick right in the face, wagging her mother's finger at him. "You got a firecracker up your rear end, just like Salvatore did," she said. "You think you can take on the whole world with your little pinky. *That's* how you're like your brother — and what does it get you? Black eyes? Stitches?"

Nick's head boiled with accusations and rebuttals he could barely keep a lid on.

"I know because I know what I see," she said. "I know what's going on with you, Nicky. I *see*."

"Mama!" shouted Paulie, sticking up for Nick for the first time in his life. "Shut up already. You're embarrassing him in front of his girlfriend."

She turned to Paulie. "You got a mouth on you, too, you know that?" She waved her mother's finger at him as well, then put it away, and looked around, ashamed of herself. "I'm sorry," she said. "You're right. I'm sorry."

Nick took three deep breaths. If he did have Sal's temper he was damn well going to control it now. "I'm taking Linda down to the cafeteria," he said. "You can meet us down there when you're done."

"Best idea I've heard all day," said his father.

Linda, already halfway out the door, took Nick's hand.

"Nicky," called his mother. Nick turned back to her

from the hallway. "Nicky." There were tears in her eyes. "You scare me, Nicky. That's all. You just scare me. . . . You just scare me."

"Mama, I'm different from Salvatore," he said. "Someday soon you're gonna see that."

And hearing that, Linda squeezed his hand so tightly his knuckles turned white.

• • •

Not a word passed between Nick and his parents on the way home. His mother and father found refuge in conversation about the heavy rain beating across the windshield, and whether or not it was safe to drive (a meaningless point, since it was clear that, short of the Great Flood, they were not going to stop).

It was dark by the time they dropped Linda off, and the rain stopped before they got home.

Once in their apartment, Nick cut a path directly for his room, but soon decided it wasn't far enough away, so he put his jacket back on and left for the roof.

When Nick heard the creaking of the old roof door hinges, he knew it must have been Marco, come to join him there.

"Whatcha doin' up here?" said Marco. "It's wet."

"I'm here for my health," snapped Nick.

Marco stepped out onto the roof, and closed the stairwell door, cutting off most of the light to the roof. "So are you still talking to me?"

Nick sighed. "Sure, why not?"

Nick hadn't spoken to Marco since Thanksgiving morning, when Marco shot off his mouth to Nick's parents about the stupid Central Park rescue. Although Nick was still mad at him, his cold shoulder was already in use with his family; he couldn't give it to Marco.

"Tough day with Salvatore?" asked Marco.

"Nah, it was fun," grumbled Nick. "We played croquet and tennis and then went to a show. What do *you* think?"

Marco looked down. "You're really good at makin' all my questions look dumb, aren't you, Nicky?"

Nick fought off the urge to say something nasty again. It was just that the taste of the afternoon lingered long after Nick left the hospital, and not even Linda's invitation to the movies could wash it away. He had turned her down, telling her he had a test to study for, which was true, though he was not about to study that night.

"Marco," asked Nick, "am I like Salvatore?"

"No way," said Marco, without a second thought. "Would Salvatore stop a mugger in Central Park and save a guy's life?"

"Salvatore would probably *be* the mugger," answered Nick.

"Prob'ly," echoed Marco.

Over in the corner, Paulie's bench press stood in a shallow puddle. Paulie had joined a health club with one of his various girlfriends, so he didn't need it anymore and had been too lazy to bring down the forgotten press for the winter. It was already starting to rust.

"So, did you tell Linda about what happened that night, and how you got the black eye?"

Nick pushed water off the vinyl seat, and lay back on the press. Marco stood behind him, ready to spot.

"Yeah, I told her," said Nick.

"Everything?"

"Everything that mattered." Nick knew what Marco was getting at.

"Did you tell her about the guy and his heart attack?"

Nick lifted the barbell out of the cradle. He heaved it up and down ten times.

"Did you tell her about the heart attack?" Marco asked again.

"There was no heart attack; the guy was just scared."

"Nicky, the guy was blue!"

"He was pale."

"Don't tell *me*, Nicky — remember, I was there!"

"So was I. More weight!" said Nick.

The fact was, the man whom Nick rescued that third night in Central Park *thought* he was having a heart attack. After Nick warded off the rather cowardly mugger (who only took two swings at Nick before running away), Nick had turned, to see that the victim was on the ground, panting. Marco, who was hiding in the bushes, stepped out and stood there gawking.

"H-h-h," the guy was saying. "H-h-heart," he said.

Nick never lost control of the situation. With the same instinct that had brought him down to the train rails months ago, Nick knelt down, opened the man's coat and shirt, and pressed his hands, one on top of the other, against the man's chest.

"H-h-heart," said the man. "Heart attack, heart attack."

Nick did not know CPR, but he had seen it on TV. Nick pushed on the man's bare chest five times hard, then waited, then pushed five times and waited again.

"Holy cow!" Marco yelled over and over again. "Holy cow!" Like Phil Rizzuto watching a string of homers fly out of the ball park.

The man seemed less tense now, but Nick pumped his chest again for good measure. It was then that Nick got a good look at the guy. Nick didn't notice if he was blue, but Nick did notice something almost too slick about him. The guy was probably some sort of hood himself.

He pushed Nick's hand off his chest, and began to button his shirt.

"Thanks, kid," he said. "For a minute I thought I was really having a coronary." He used Nick's shoulder to help himself up.

Still shaky, the man wiped some cold sweat from his brow, tried to catch his breath, looked around furtively, then reached into his pocket.

"Here's for you and your friend." He tossed a bill at them. "Thanks," he said, and hobbled off weakly into the shadows of the park. The bill was a fifty.

"You could make a regular living at this," Marco had commented on the way home. But then, what would it matter if all his parents could see were the black eyes and stitches?

"More weight," said Nick, and Marco obediently slipped some more weights on the sides of the barbell. Nick lifted it five times before his left arm began to buckle. Marco helped it back into the cradle.

"More weight," said Nick again.

"But Nicky —"

"You heard me."

Marco did the job, and Nick hefted the overloaded barbell from the cradle. Nick gritted his teeth. The barbell came down slowly to his chest, then he pressed up with all his might. This was for his mother and for Salvatore. This was for Paulie, who was so much smarter than Nick, and always letting him know it. This was for Linda, who didn't believe in the rescues. This was for everybody.

The barbell labored up and, with a profound aching in his arms, Nick dropped it into the cast-iron cradle.

"More weight," he said.

Marco hesitated. "There *is* no more weight, Nicky," he said, and Nick let out a sigh of relief. He sat up and looked at his hands, icy cold and red from the barbell. He rubbed them together, feeling where blisters would rise the next day.

He had pressed more weight than Paulie or Salvatore had ever pressed. It was just like his rescues, now. He could do anything he set his mind to, couldn't he? He couldn't lose.

Nick shook his arms, trying to work out the knots in his biceps. Marco watched him and then looked away. Something was troubling him.

"You know . . . that guy *did* have a heart attack, Nicky," said Marco.

"Don't be stupid."

"I'm not stupid," said Marco. "For once I'm not." Marco stared at Nick unblinking, riveted. Nick didn't like it.

"If he had a heart attack," said Nick, "then how could he just up and walk away like that?"

Marco shrugged. "That's easy. You healed him."

The knots in Nick's arms seemed to tighten. Marco waited anxiously for his reaction. "You're an A-one, certified lunatic!" said Nick. "You know that?" Nick tried to shake the thought off his back, but Marco wasn't making it easy. He was quite certain of his conclusions.

"If you're so sure I'm wrong about it," said Marco, "why don't you flip a coin over it?"

He reached into his pocket and pulled out an ordinary quarter, tarnished black in the crevices, covered with pocket lint. He held it out to Nick.

"No," said Nick. Plain and simple. "No."

"Why not?" Marco held out the coin like a stranger offering candy. "What are you afraid of?"

Nick swallowed, and a sense of dread began to fill him.

"No," said Nick again, and slapped the quarter out of Marco's hand. It disappeared over the side of the roof. "Get the hell out of here," said Nick.

Marco nodded. "I'll be downstairs watching TV if you want to come down," he said, and sauntered to the stairwell.

"You ought to be happy about it," added Marco. "If it was me who healed the guy, *I'd* be pretty happy about it." He shook his head. "How come *you* always get all the luck?"

Marco opened the door and left, letting Bozo the cat onto the roof to scamper happily around. Nick fought the urge to kick the stupid cat off the roof.

11 · A Balanced Equation

Two miles away, and a few hundred feet closer to the clouds, Linda lay awake in her bedroom cursing the incessant ticking of her antique clock.

Nick had barely spoken to her after his fight with his mother in Salvatore's hospital room. Linda and Nick rode down in the elevator together, then sat and had some stale hospital muffins at the cafeteria, but Nick wasn't really there. He was simmering away, deep in his own private anger, and Linda was still so freaked out by coming face-to-face with Nick's "dead" brother, she wasn't quite prepared to help Nick sort things through.

The fact was, Nick *did* look like Salvatore, and seeing him with her own eyes was a horrifying thing. It seemed a portent of things to come, and Linda understood exactly what Nick's mom had meant about Nick's rescues, even if Mrs. Herrera hadn't said it in the most tactful and eloquent of terms.

Linda couldn't tell Nick any of that, and so she said nothing. She ate her dry muffin and talked about how bad hospital food was. She even went so far as to make up a story about how poorly she had been treated at the hospital when she had her tonsils out, just so she would have something to say. The fact was, her tonsils were still firmly attached to her throat, and she had never actually stayed in a hospital.

Nick then went on to tell her about some aunt who was accidentally labeled deceased during a stay at Bellevue. Linda suspected he made that one up as well because lying was better than not saying anything at all.

The clock ticked away, and Linda shoved her head beneath her pillow.

Trying to deal with Nick was like trying to solve the most complex of algebraic equations, and the more deeply involved she got, the more variables seemed to pop up to confuse her.

But she had yet to come across an equation that she couldn't solve . . . eventually.

Her first thought had been to forbid Nick from performing rescues. She could threaten him, saying, "If you ever perform another rescue, *ever* again, I will *never* speak to you for the rest of your life."

But what if he chose the rescues over her? Or worse, what if he gave up the rescues and hated her for making him do it? Clearly it was a wrong solution.

She could try to approach him logically, and bombard him with a dozen arguments that made perfect sense, proving that his rescues were governed by the same laws that ruled the rest of the universe — that his coin trick came about as a rare but possible event, like winning the lottery, or perhaps it was even simpler than that: perhaps Nick had become so mechanically adept at flipping a coin that somehow he could catch it exactly the same way each time he flipped it.

But Nick wasn't buying it. As far as he was concerned, logic had lost the battle long ago.

The clock chimed midnight. Linda swung herself out of bed, grabbed the heavy clock, and practically threw it into the back of her closet. The last three pitiful chimes of midnight were muffled by the closet door as she closed it.

She dived back on her bed and growled in frustration. But she knew frustration would not help her. It was as useless an emotion as fear. And so she rolled over and lay flat on her back, relaxing her feet, then her legs, and let the relaxation flow through the rest of her body.

Patience, she told herself. *Have patience;* the solution will come. If she thought it through calmly, she'd have it all worked out by morning — she knew that — for there was never an equation that defied solution. Never. And knowing that made her feel much better.

Yes, she would have her solution. She would be the one to rescue Nick from his own rescues. Everything would be under control.

12 · *Who You Gonna Call?*

And miraculously, the rescues began to fall right at Nick's feet once every couple of weeks. Perhaps the opportunities had always been there before, but until that fateful day in the subway, he never raised his eyes to look for them. Now he had developed a keen eye and acute reflexes to take charge of any potential disaster that arose. And the best part about it was that Linda was usually there to witness his acts of courage. If she was a doubter of his ability before, surely she could not doubt now.

The fact was, Linda took up all of his free time now. Since her school let out fifteen minutes before his, she would always be there waiting for him by his side entrance. She had taken to tutoring him, for she happened to get a glimpse of his faltering grades.

"I refuse to go out with someone who can't get past the tenth grade," she said, one-quarter joking, and three-quarters serious.

Linda spent so much time with Nick that he couldn't go looking for his own rescues even if he wanted to. But fortunately he didn't need to anymore.

•   •   •

The next one came on a cold Sunday, about two weeks before Christmas.

He and Linda stopped at Nathan's World Famous Coney Island Hot Dogs after a movie. Halfway through their meal, Nick heard a commotion a few tables away. A girl of eighteen or nineteen had begun to choke on her World Famous Coney Island Hot Dog. She stood, her hands flailing wildly in the air.

"She's choking!" announced Linda. "Somebody do something!"

Nick was quick to his feet — but not quick enough.

"Out of my way," said a man, pushing Nick aside. "I'm a doctor."

But in the commotion, he accidentally tripped over Linda's foot and went sprawling onto the floor. Nick reached the choking victim first.

"The Heimlich maneuver," yelled a man from the next table, who was more than happy just to watch with his legs crossed. Nick picked up the girl, and tried to give her what he believed was the Heimlich maneuver. He grabbed her from behind and punched her in the stomach. She groaned and fell on the floor.

"Give her mouth-to-mouth," said an old woman with a cigarette dangling from her upper lip.

Nick knelt down and prepared to give her mouth-to-mouth resuscitation.

"No!" yelled the doctor, just getting back to his feet. "That's not what you do for a choking victim!"

Nevertheless, Nick resuscitated the girl three times, and on the third time, she coughed, expelling a chunk of her World Famous Coney Island Hot Dog into the air.

She began breathing in gasps.

"You . . . You . . . saved . . . saved my life," she said.

"But," said the doctor, "that's not what you do for a choking victim."

Yet it had worked and the girl had been saved.

"Hey," said the old woman with the cigarette. She wagged a finger at Nick. "I know you! I seen ya on TV. Aren't you Nick Herrera?" But Linda pulled him away from the scene and out into the street before he had a chance to answer.

On the ride home, Nick was all smiles. Saving a life had never been so easy.

• • •

Then there was another incident, as quick, and almost as easy, as the first.

Nick dragged an unconscious sewer worker from the bowels of the earth, after the worker had been practically suffocated by noxious fumes. The fumes didn't bother Nick in the least, although he wasn't too pleasant to smell after the incident and Linda insisted he buy an entire new outfit at the nearest clothing store.

• • •

Yet another opportunity presented itself one night right around New Year's. When Nick and Linda emerged from a Broadway theater, Nick caught two unsavory-looking thugs mugging an old woman in a side alley. Nick intervened quickly. Muggings were already old hat to Nick.

Although the thugs were bigger than he, Nick was able to knock one of them down into a row of trash-cans, and scare the other away. The second thug aimed a gun as he ran, but he didn't have the guts to shoot. Nick returned the purse to the woman, and rejoined Linda, who had tried in vain to get help. She fussed over him and kept asking him if he was OK.

Nick was more than OK — he felt invigorated and electrified.

He couldn't lose! It was becoming clearer and clearer. If all his rescues became so easy, he'd have it made.

On the cab ride home that night, Linda leaned in close to him. "I'm glad for you," she told him. "If it makes you happy, then I hope you get to rescue everyone in the world."

It was a complete turnaround, and her change of heart was remarkable. Her doubts and worries had dissolved away completely, and it fed Nick's confidence. If Linda believed that the odds had been rigged in his favor, then it really must be true. Not even the Steroid Avenger led such a charmed life!

Of course, none of those three rescues made the news, yet it seemed people found out about them anyway, because Nick had a habit of telling Marco, and Marco, who was the gossip king of the Upper East Side, had a habit of notifying the rest of humanity.

In a matter of days, Marco's network of gossip and rumors was moving through the tangled grapevine of the city like a fast-growing weed. It took root everywhere, like crabgrass in the sidewalk.

The tales grew taller by the minute, and often, when they came back to Nick they were so distorted he barely recognized them. According to several sources, Nick had fended off four muggers with semiautomatic weapons, Nick had dragged a dying man through miles of sewers, battling alligators and rats, and Nick had delivered a woman's baby in the kitchen of Nathan's World Famous Coney Island Hot Dogs. Someone actually came up to Nick and asked him if it was true he had defused a terrorist bomb, and when he told them "No," they refused to believe him!

Well, if that was what people wanted to believe, Nick decided to let them believe it, for Nick knew what was fact and what was fiction.

Or at least he thought he did.

These rumors made it back to Nick, but the very strongest rumors never came his way. They were spoken in hushed whispers that passed around him, above him, and below him, as invisible as radiation.

No one dared to ask Nick about those rumors, and so he never knew just how far the gears he had set in motion had turned, and how very large those gears had grown.

He knew nothing about it, until the night Marco called him at Linda's.

•　•　•

It was a week into the New Year. The night was frigid — fifteen degrees — and the air seemed charged with an icy tension so still that the city could have been floating in space.

Nick sat with Linda in her living room that evening, drudging through trigonometry and sipping fresh-squeezed orange juice from elegant Waterford crystal champagne glasses. This lesson was part of her crusade to raise his grades enough to get him into her exclusive school — a school with a tuition Nick couldn't afford anyway.

His studies had been going reasonably well, but tonight Nick's mind was somewhere outside, thinking about the night and whether or not the stillness was a prelude to a blizzard. Nick listened and couldn't even hear the wind in the elevator shafts tonight.

"Soh-Cah-Toa?" asked Linda, as she leafed through her notes.

"Excuse me?"

"Soh-Cah-Toa. What does it mean?" she asked.

Nick couldn't care less. He stood and crossed the room to the window, looking out, but not down. He touched the thick glass, and it felt so cold it seemed to drain half the heat from his body. The solid white cloud cover hung suspended above the city like the iron grid above the Carnegie Hall stage, looking impossibly heavy. Nick imagined that the entire sky could come crashing down at any minute, shattering the city like Linda's tray of fine Waterford crystal.

"Soh . . . Soh-Cah . . . What?"

"Soh . . . Cah . . . Toa," repeated Linda impatiently. "We've gone over this before."

Nick was slowly beginning to feel an unnerving and inexplicable sense of dread. It reminded him of the night of their near-disastrous flight.

"Are you listening to me?" asked Linda.

Perhaps it was the altitude. Perhaps it was bad pâté.

"C'mon," said Linda, impatiently brushing her thick red hair. "I've got my own homework to do, and I can't help you all night."

Nick looked at her blankly.

"Each letter stands for something," said Linda. "It's a trick to help you remember trig: S-O-H, C-A-H, T-O-A."

"Sine . . . ," said Nick, ". . . Cosine . . . Hypotenuse . . ."

"Ugghhh!" Linda downed her orange juice and poured herself another glass. "What's wrong with you?" she said. "I know you're not *that* dense."

The phone rang less than a minute later, and Linda answered it.

"Good God," said Linda, covering the mouthpiece. "It's Marco. How did he get this number?" She handed the phone to Nick. "As your tutor, I suggest you get rid of him so you can study for your test," she said. "As your girlfriend, I suggest you get rid of him, period."

Nick took the phone. "Marco?"

"Thank God I got you!" Marco whispered into the phone as though he was calling from behind enemy lines.

"What's up?"

"You got this call," whispered Marco. "I was over at your house eating your dinner — on account of you didn't come home to eat, and your mom hates to waste good food — when all of a sudden the phone rings. Your mom picks it up and it's for you, and she figures it's one of our friends, you know, from school, so she asks if I want to talk to him, and I say sure. So I scarf down the rest of my lasagna real fast and —"

"Marco, get to the point."

By now Linda had crossed the room and picked up another extension.

"Yeah," says Marco. "So the guy isn't from school but he says he's gotta talk to you anyway, and do I know where you are. He says it's an emergency and he can't talk to no one else but you."

"So," said Nick, "did you get a number?"

"No," said Marco. "He said he has to see you. Tonight."

"Sorry," said Linda, as if she were Nick's mother. "He's got a math test tomorrow, and he's studying."

"Yeah, I know," said Marco, "but this guy's not gonna wait. He's at 1830 Columbus Avenue."

"He'll be there a long time," said Linda, ready to hang up.

"No he won't!" said Marco. "That's what I'm trying to tell you. He says he's gonna be waiting for Nicky up on the roof, and he sounded kind of weird about it. . . ."

Nick didn't get the big picture quite yet, but it was beginning to dawn on him.

"Nicky, I think this guy's gonna jump. You're the only person he'll talk to, and I think he's gonna jump. You gotta stop him."

Nick's sense of dread blossomed into horror. He could almost hear the sky crashing down upon the fragile crystal of the city.

"No," said Linda, slamming down her receiver and striding across the room toward Nick. "I won't let you!"

"Why does he want me?" Nick asked Marco, but he knew the answer even before Marco told him.

"Because you're the one, Nicky," said Marco, plainly and simply. "People know you now — you're like a household word. . . . If you needed saving who would *you* want to talk to?"

"You can't let people use you like this!" Linda screamed in his other ear, determined not to let him go.

But what choice did Nick have?

"Who knows about this?" Nick asked Marco.

"Just us," he said.

"Good," said Nick. "Keep it that way." Nick hung up the phone, and seriously considered his course of action.

"This guy is gonna jump anyway!" pleaded Linda. "Whether he talks to you or not! What if he's a psycho? What if he has a gun?"

What if, what if, what if! "So I should let him jump?" yelled Nick back at her.

"It's not your responsibility," she pleaded.

But she was wrong. It *was* his responsibility.

Nick grabbed his coat off the couch and put it on.

"You're afraid of heights," she cruelly reminded him.

"Used to be," he calmly corrected. Nick went to the front closet, pulled out one of Linda's countless coats and tossed it to her. She stood there, clasping the thick fur in her hands.

"What about your test?" she said weakly. She was out of ammunition, and she looked frazzled and frightened. Why was she so concerned now? Had she lost faith in him?

"*S*ine equals *O*pposite over *H*ypotenuse," said Nick. "*C*osine equals *A*djacent over *H*ypotenuse. *T*angent equals *O*pposite over *A*djacent. Soh-Cah-Toa."

Nick opened the front door. "Are you coming or not?"

13 · *The Leaper*

Flurries had already started falling, dropping lightly through the windless night. While it was not the first snow of the winter, it was the first one that looked as though it would stick. A fine layer of white already dusted the sidewalk.

Nick arrived at the West Side building five minutes ahead of Linda. They had started out together, but the cab got stuck in a quagmire of traffic on Fifty-seventh Street and Nick had left it, setting out on foot.

As the address numbers on Columbus Avenue got higher and higher, Nick's fear grew stronger. At the last few rescues he had felt powerful and completely in control. This time, he just felt sick.

Nick knew which building it was even before he saw the address, because dozens of people stood out front. He hadn't expected anyone else to know about the leaper, but he should have known better. There were spectators, some cops, and one news crew that Nick could see. Marco must have called the whole world to alert them of Nick's next rescue — but the last thing Nick wanted tonight was a press agent.

The news crew saw him and recognized him. Although they weren't set up for broadcasting yet, they tried to pull him aside for an interview. Nick walked right past them, toward the front door of the building. The leaper would be on the roof, and Nick did not want to waste time.

It was his father who stopped him.

Joe Herrera stood right in front of the doorway, still in uniform, blocking Nick's entrance into the building. The reporters didn't bother with Officer Herrera, because they knew he didn't give interviews about his son anymore. As Nick approached, the expression on his father's face was grave and cold. He hadn't seen or spoken to his father very much at all lately, and now the distance between them seemed immense when they stood so close.

"Congratulations," his father said in no kind tone. "Now you've got yourself a fan club, and this *pendejo* on the roof must be the president." He took a step closer to Nick, and spoke slowly and forcefully.

"I don't want you to go up there," said his father. "But it seems I have no say in the matter." Nick couldn't find the words to say to his father, and he wondered how long it had been since Nick *could* speak to him.

"You talk to this guy from far away," ordered his father. "Do you understand me? You do not get anywhere near the edge of that roof . . . and if he climbs out onto the ledge, you don't go near him. You let him jump. Is that understood?"

He waited for an answer. Nick nodded, and his father took a step back.

"Go talk to this son-of-a-bitch, and get this thing over with." He moved aside so Nick could pass, then turned away, unable to watch Nick enter the building.

In the lobby, Nick was met by a shrink and two cops, who tried to give Nick a full course in the psychology of leapers as the elevator took them up to the eighteenth floor — just beneath the roof.

"Keep him talking," they told Nick. "Remember, most leapers want to be talked down, and since he asked for you, he'll probably listen to you. What are you, a friend of his?"

Nick shook his head.

"Well, talk to him like you are. Tell him what you think he wants to hear, and whatever you do, don't be a hero. The last thing we need are *two* dead kids on our hands."

Nick's stomach leapt as the elevator stopped suddenly and the doors slid open.

On the top floor, people peered out of their apartment doors. Down at the end of the hall, beyond the steel fire door, a few policemen milled about aimlessly.

"He won't let us get near him," said a cop. "Maybe you'll have better luck."

And then the bad news.

"He just climbed out onto the ledge."

How high were they? Eighteen floors. A three-story fire escape was easy. A six-story roof was easy. He'd even been able to handle the grid, but an eighteen-story ledge? As he climbed the stairs to the roof, the feeling of dread almost made him lose his balance, and when he opened the door, he felt as if he were jumping to the tracks of the subway again. This should have been just routine for him. It should have been easy, but the fear wouldn't leave him.

Nick slowly made his way across the gravel roof, toward the edge of the building. The building's architect, with infinite wisdom, had called for a lip about three and a half feet high at the edge, to keep stupid people from falling off, but it was not high enough to prevent determined people from climbing over. Just on the other side of the brick guard was a concrete ledge no more than two feet wide.

Way down the ledge was someone wearing a blue woolen ski mask over his entire face. Nick, not daring to climb over to the ledge, walked toward him, and peered over the edge just a few feet away. The ski mask turned to look at him.

"You bastard," said the leaper. "You didn't have to tell the whole world. This was supposed to be a simple conversation, just me and you. You blew it, pal!"

The voice was young. Maybe his age.

"I didn't tell," said Nick. "Someone else did."

The leaper turned his gaze to the city, not really listening to Nick. "I just wanted to talk, that's all, and now look what it's turned into. Now it's goddamned NEWS. Does everything you do *have* to be news?"

Nick didn't answer that. "Do you really want to jump?" asked Nick.

The leaper shrugged. "If I don't I'll be disappointing all the spectators, won't I?" The voice was hoarse, as if he had done a lot of screaming or crying, or something. His hands were shaking, and Nick figured he was cold, or scared, or on drugs, or all three.

"You're just gonna stand there, aren't you," said the

leaper, "trying to convince me to come down; is that it?"

"What am I supposed to do?" asked Nick. "I'm still sort of new at this stuff, OK?" None of Nick's rescues had required talking. This was a first.

The leaper rubbed his eye through his mask. "I put this mask on when the cops showed up," he said, "because I didn't want them to know who I was." He waited for a reaction from Nick, but got none.

"You still don't know who I am, do you?" asked the leaper.

Nick thought he might have recognized the voice, but he wasn't sure. He shook his head.

"Well, said the leaper reaching for his mask, "I guess this thing doesn't matter now anyway. They're gonna find out." He took off the mask, threw it off the ledge, and turned his face to Nick. Nick nearly lost his balance.

Max Barbett stared back at Nick from the ledge. Nick let out a huge breath of steam in surprise.

"Pretty amazing, huh?"

Max didn't look much like the same person who'd been at Linda's party. His eyes were wild and red. His hair was a staticky mess from the mask.

Max didn't ask Nick to come out on the ledge with him. Nick didn't even like Max, but there was that desperation in Max's face, and well, if Nick's father had seen that desperation, maybe he would have let Nick climb out after him. And maybe not.

But Nick did it anyway.

Holding on tight to the three-foot wall, Nick scrambled over onto the slippery, rime-covered edge. Flurries still drifted downward, and although there was no wind to make him lose his balance, it felt as if he and the wall were two mismatched magnets repelling each other.

"You're not very good at this, are you?" said Max.

Nick had to sit down right away, or he felt sure he would be repelled right off the side. The seat of his pants melted a thin layer of damp snow, and it soaked right through. He closed his eyes for a moment, and when he opened them again, it seemed to him as if the rest of the world had vanished. There was nothing now. Nothing but Nick, Max, and the ledge.

"Is this some kind of joke?" asked Nick.

"You're an asshole if you really think that," said Max.

"Well, if you're gonna off yourself, why do you need me here?"

He threw Nick a nasty gaze. "Because there's a lot of things you don't know." He cracked his shaky knuckles, and rolled his neck to get a kink out of it.

"The Olympics are over, so you don't have to dive anymore," offered Nick. "And don't give me that crap about how you can't stop. If you don't like diving, then don't do it."

Max laughed. "You think that's what this is all about? Water sports?"

Nick didn't say anything more. Obviously Max took everything he said as the words of an idiot.

After a long, cold while, Max began to talk.

"It's not fair," he said, and teardrops came with his words. He wasn't sobbing or anything, but the tears flowed in a steady stream. He looked much younger when he cried. He sounded much younger.

Max stood up and took a step closer to the edge. Nick could not as much as move from where he sat.

"I told you about my cousin who croaked, right? What I didn't tell you is that he had pains just like mine before he went belly-up. He was athletic too." He took a moment to wipe his nose.

"So, maybe it's just in your head," suggested Nick.

"So, maybe it's not," said Max. "Like, maybe I've got what he had; a thinning of the ventricle walls, and maybe it's a genetic defect, and maybe the doctors have put me through all the tests and they know that it's true. Did you ever think of that?"

Max now stood at the very edge of the ledge, his back to the city, in perfect posture. "And maybe I've known for a while."

It was clear to Nick that Max was preparing for a dive, but Nick didn't dare move an inch.

"A genetic defect!" said Max. "Can you believe that? I got three gold medals. I've been on the cover of *Time* magazine twice! Genetic defect!"

Max stretched his arms out as he would before a dive, taking a moment to balance himself. "Now they tell me I'll probably die if I don't get this open-heart surgery — which one in three people survive — so I'll die anyway, right? . . . and I *don't* want to die on a damn operating table."

Max took some time to catch his breath. This must have been what Max wouldn't say when they were playing truths there in Bobby's plane. What a frightening thing to live with!

"I always wondered," said Max, "how controlled a dive could be from this high, you know?" He rose up on his toes, and whatever else about him was off-balanced, he was able to balance himself perfectly on the tip of that ledge. "A sextuple gainer, with a quadruple twist. There's one for Guinness, huh?"

Nick grimaced, waiting in silence for the moment Max would take the plunge.

"Don't be such a woosie," said Max. He put his hands down, and casually stepped away from the ledge, sitting down next to Nick once more, like it was nothing.

"So what am I here for?" asked Nick, angrily. "Am I supposed to give you a score?"

"Stop the crap," said Max. "You know why you're here."

But Nick still waited for an explanation.

Max looked at his shaking hands and sat on them. His eye was twitching a bit. He tried to blink it out. "I saw what happened on that plane," said Max. "Remember? I was there."

Nick thought back to their ill-fated joyride. When it came to the rescues, Max had been the biggest skeptic of them all.

"I can't rescue people who don't have enough sense to come in off a ledge."

"If you could land that plane, you can help me."

"Bobby landed the plane, not me," said Nick. "Nothing happened. You said it yourself."

"Yeah, that's what I said, but I've had a good long time to think about it since then." Max shivered and looked at Nick with wild eyes. "You're gonna tell me that your coin flip was just a trick?"

Nick didn't answer that.

"No, I didn't think so."

But Nick knew Max hadn't called him because of the coin flip. There was something more. Nick was filled with a renewed sense of terror. He didn't want to hear what Max had in mind.

"It's not just rescues, is it?" asked Max.

"I have no idea what you're talking about."

"I know what I saw!" said Max. "And I know what I've heard!"

Nick watched Max in disbelief, as he would watch a friend slowly pull a gun from his coat pocket and aim it at him. Max unzipped his jacket, and unbuttoned his shirt in the frigid night, revealing a bare chest already filling with goosebumps.

"I want you to heal me, too . . . ," said Max, ". . . like that man who had the heart attack in the park . . . and all those others."

Nick's soul rolled with a wave of nausea.

"You're insane!" said Nick. "You're on drugs!"

"I know what I saw!" Max gritted his teeth and they began to chatter. "And I know what I've heard. There are too many people talking about it for it *all* to be lies!"

Nick felt dizzy, and suddenly the whole world, which had blinked out a moment before, blinked back in with sparkling clarity. The unfeeling lights of the city. The snow falling past them to the earth almost two hundred feet below. The sirens, the crowds. Nick could feel the building repelling him toward the edge again.

Nick stood in a panic, and his feet slipped out from under him, skidding on the white rime of the ledge. He did a half-turn and, grabbing onto the brick lip, he used all his strength to hurl himself over the three-foot guard, back onto the roof. When he felt his shoulder come down on the sharp gravel and he knew he was safe, only then did he turn back to Max.

"I guess it was all lies," murmured Max, "but it was worth a shot." Max stood on the very edge of the ledge again, his back to the city once more. "I refuse to die on an operating table."

He stood on his toes, and stretched out his arms, ready to do his record-shattering dive to the hard pavement. "I'll be a cinch for the cover of *Sports Illustrated*," he said. "Maybe even a whole special issue."

"No!" Nick reached out to him, but would not get near that ledge again. Nick didn't blink, for fear that if he did, he'd open his eyes to find Max no longer there.

"I'll do it!" yelled Nick. Max looked at him, still standing on his toes. "I'll do it."

"Is it true then?" said Max.

"Yes, all of it!" said Nick. "I can heal people. I've healed dozens of people — hundreds of 'em. Hearts are my specialty."

Max took a step away from the ledge, almost laughing. He was delirious. "Then I'm not nuts," he said. He looked even more wired than before. He must be *on* something, Nick decided. He had to be.

Behind Nick, the police came racing through the doorway as they saw Max begin to climb over the brick guard wall, to safety.

"Jeez!" Nick heard one of them say. "Is that Max Barbett?"

"Come on over here," said Nick. "So I can heal you and we can forget about this." Nick reached out his hand, about four feet away from Max's bare chest. If Max wanted to be healed he'd have to come to Nick.

Max seemed to half believe him and half not — but half was enough. He stepped over the low wall, onto the gravel roof, and as he did, police seemed to appear from everywhere and surrounded him. They grabbed Max with a dozen hands, as if they would tear him apart, but Max didn't care about that yet. "Where's Herrera?" he asked. "Where is he?"

But Nick was already far, far away.

• • •

Out in the street, Nick brushed past his father and the reporters, cutting a direct path to Marco, who stood a measured distance away from Linda. The crowd, which had grown, cheered as they saw him, but Nick completely ignored that.

"Good goin'!" said Marco. "Knew you could do it!"

Nick grabbed Marco by the neck, pushing him back into a mailbox. The box echoed a dull thud.

"What have you been telling people?" asked Nick.

Marco stuttered for a moment. "Nothing," said Marco. "Nothing!" Marco knocked Nick's hand away. "Get your hands off me."

"I can heal people; is that what you told them?"

"You can!" insisted Marco. "You know it. You're just too dense and stubborn to admit it."

"Just because *one* guy *thinks* he has a heart attack . . ."

"It's not just that," said Marco. "What about your father's limp?"

"Huh?"

"Your father walked with a limp, didn't he? Have you noticed he doesn't anymore?"

"No, but —"

"And what about Bozo? That cat was dying — wasn't it? Now look at the thing," yelled Marco.

"I never touched that cat!"

"Bull! I always see you petting it on the fire escape!"

By now Linda had made her way over and was watching the battle.

Marco was hitting Nick with too much, too fast. Nick didn't know what to say. "You're a first-class moron!" he blurted. Nick tried to grab Marco again, but Marco deflected his hand.

"You call me whatever you want," said Marco, "but it doesn't change a thing."

Nick found himself reaching up to cover his ears.

"The light's been shining in your face, but you don't even see it, Nicky," said Marco. "You're like a psychic who goes to séances and stuff when he should be betting big money at the races!"

"Nick," said Linda, desperately trying to pull him away. "There's your dad. Go with him. Now!"

"Don't you see?" said Marco. "All this time you figured you're supposed to be rescuing people, when all along, you could have been healing people instead!"

Nick took a moment to catch his breath. He didn't want to hear this. As usual, Marco had put two and two together and come up with seventeen.

"You can't take him seriously?" said Linda, dismissing the whole thing quickly and completely. Nick wanted to dismiss it as well, but it wasn't as easy for him, and that made him angry. He could feel the anger welling up inside of him, reaching out toward his fists.

It was then they brought Max out of the building. He caught sight of Nick and went wild, but the police held him back.

"He said he'd heal me!" screamed Max. "He said he'd heal me!"

And from that moment on, Nick knew his public image and indeed, his entire life had taken an awful turn. A murmur passed through the crowd, settling with the reporters, who turned to Nick and began to approach him. More than likely they didn't believe it in the least, but that didn't matter. It made good reading.

"Nicky," said Marco, "if I could do what you can do, I'd be rich! I'd have my own TV show! I'd . . ."

Nick couldn't hold back any longer. "You *stupid* son-of-a-bitch!" and for the first time in his life, Nick threw a heavy fist right at Marco's face. Marco's head flung sharply with the punch, which connected right with his eye. He stumbled but didn't fall. Nick would have gone after him again if it hadn't been for the reporters around him. They didn't seem to care about the fight. All they wanted to know was what had happened up there on the ledge. And what was this about healing? What was all this about?

Marco looked at Nick like a wounded bear. He didn't lift a hand to Nick.

"That's OK, Nicky," he said slowly. "I know it's just because you're upset."

Nick couldn't look at him anymore — he couldn't look at any of them — and so he ran.

• • •

Linda caught up with him in an alley, two blocks away. Nick felt like throwing up, but just couldn't get himself to. What he wanted out was not in his stomach.

"Listen to me, Nick," said Linda, grabbing his head in her hands so tightly her nails almost dug into his temples.

"Max is crazy, and Marco's an imbecile," she said. "I, on the other hand, am a sensible and rational human being. *That's* the only 'light' that should be shining in your face," she said, mimicking Marco.

"Don't you think I know that?" Nick grabbed her hands and threw them off of his face.

"Then what's the problem?" asked Linda. "You just go back there and deny it," she said, as if it was all that simple.

"It doesn't matter what I say!" said Nick. "People are gonna hear what they want to hear anyway. They're gonna hear whatever those reporters write. And did you see the looks on their faces? They were like a pack of wolves!"

Linda took a moment to think this out. "OK," she said. "Then you just go back there and you lay your hands on Max, or whatever it is you have to do, and prove to the world that you can't heal him, or anybody!"

Nick pulled away from her.

"No!" said Nick. "I can't do that." He would not go near Max on a bet now. He would not go near Max for all the money in the world.

"Why not?"

"Linda, just go away," he said, pushing her away from him. "Just leave me alone!" He ran out of the alley, moving so swiftly that he lost control on the slick sidewalk, and smashed into a parking meter, nearly breaking a rib.

Nick got up and looked at the mindless little parking meter with its red violation flag up. He kicked it as hard as he could. Stupid thing. Damn stupid thing. Friggin' stupid thing. He kicked it again and again, and finally its face exploded, throwing quarters, dimes, and nickels across the dusting of snow on the pavement.

And Nick hurried off, refusing to look down, for fear that the light shining in his face would be the glow of every nickel, every dime, and every quarter showing heads.

• • •

Nick went straight for his room, passing his mother, who sat in the living room watching TV — probably the news report he had just run from. When she saw him, she hoisted herself up and came after him.

"Nicky!" she said. "I gotta talk to you." There was a warble in her voice. Nick reached his room, closed the door, and locked it from the inside.

"I'm going to sleep," he told her. "Leave me alone." She knocked a few times, called his name, and finally gave up.

In the morning, the city would know what happened. Nick would be the joke of the town, and the saint of some self-appointed lunatic disciples. There were thousands of Marcos in the city. Thousands of people as desperate as Max. If only one in one hundred believed, Nick would have sixty thousand followers by morning.

He looked at his hands. They were red from the cold. Yes, those hands had come through for him in the rescues, but they were nothing more than normal everyday hands. They felt pain. They wrote sloppily and occasionally bobbled fly balls in softball. They were normal; they didn't glow, they didn't pulsate with a magnetic aura or anything. How could anyone believe. . . ?"

Nick looked up to see he was not alone. Bozo was sitting on the dresser, regarding him curiously.

Nick grabbed a Bible that his mother had so carefully left open for him on his desk and hurled it at the little beast. The cat screeched and flew off the dresser like a cat ten years younger, dodging the swiftly flying Bible, which hit the wall with a thud.

In the corner Bozo cowered, wondering what her unpredictable owner would do next. Nick tried to shoo the cat out of the room, but it would not go. It just kept running under his desk and under his bed, and into his closet. If he wanted it out, he would have to carry it out.

He reached under the bed, grabbed the cat and pulled it out. The cat fussed until Nick had it cradled gently in his arms. It sniffed his hands, and looked up at him.

He could very easily strangle the thing now. Break its neck. It was in his power to do so — and then he could tell Marco that the thing had died, just as everyone said it would because it was old and sick. Nothing special about this cat. Nothing at all.

Bozo stared at Nick with sharp yellow cat eyes. He could do it, and end the nonsense once and for all. . . .

With one hand Nick opened the door, and with the other he tossed the cat out into the hallway. It scampered away and into Paulie's room.

Then he closed his door and closed out the world.

And as Nick lay on his bed and shut his eyes, he began to realize something. He began to understand why he was still so terribly uptight, and why he just couldn't let the miserable evening go. Nick was, in a way, still on that ledge with Max — he had never come down. Yes, Linda was right, Nick could touch

Max, and Max would be no better off than be-fore. . . .

. . . But what if he touched Max, and Max was healed? What if this once, two and two did add up to seventeen? *What if?* Surely the chances of it were next to impossible, but what if it happened?

That would be like taking a leap off of that ledge and flying instead of falling.

What if? Surely it would be too much for his mind to stand. He would simply snap and end up locked away in the rubber room of King's County's lunatic tower, screaming at the moon.

He couldn't risk that, and the only other choice he could see right now was to simply stay on that ledge, and never find out. He would never talk about it, he would never think about it . . . and he would never attempt to heal anyone. Ever.

14 · Waiting for the Paper

Nick didn't hear his father come home. He must have slipped in during one of the brief moments Nick had slipped off into sleep that night.

The city was beginning to stretch itself awake when, at five, Nick ventured out into the cool wooden floor for a trip to the john.

On his way back, he caught sight of his father sitting in the living room, wrapped neck to toe in a big old comforter. The soft blue light of the television played on his face. Nick stayed in the shadows for fear that his father was angry at him. After all, he had disobeyed his orders and stepped out on the ledge. But Mr. Herrera saw Nick and beckoned him to come.

"*Venga aquí*," said his father. "*Siéntate*, Nicky." It was the first time his father had used such a kind tone with him for weeks. Nick came over and sat down on the large sofa, and his father flung the old comforter around him as well.

For a brief moment Nick felt the relief of forgetting the world. He could have been seven years old then. That was perhaps the last time they had spent a cold morning together under the comforter in front of the television set. Usually they had watched an ancient film or a ridiculous agriculture show, talking of crops and "animal husbandry," which Nick found particularly amusing. Those shows portrayed a strange and exotic farming culture that, to him, might as well have been on Mars.

But now his father watched something else. Something Nick had seen before.

A baby in his mother's arms. A four-year-old boy in the sand, building castles. A nine-year-old making rude faces at the camera, and running back and forth. They had put their old home movies on video about two years ago, but rarely watched it.

"Do you remember this trip, Nicky?"

Nick shrugged apologetically. "I was one year old," he said.

His mother waved at the camera. The washed-out colors of the film made her seem pale. Even when Nick saw it with his own eyes, he could not imagine her ever having been that young.

Salvatore danced a hula across the screen, and ran off.

"Such a ham," said his father. He watched the video for a few minutes longer, without even blinking. Then he got up to get a drink. He moved so easily and casually, it brought back to Nick the uneasiness of the night before.

"Dad . . . ," said Nick, as his father sat back down on the couch, "you're not limping today."

His father shrugged. "It comes and goes, Nicky, it comes and goes." He took a sip of his juice.

"How long since you last limped?"

But his father just shrugged again. "The doctors said one day it would just go away, and I wouldn't even notice it. They were right."

Nick nodded, and watched the video for at least a minute before he spoke again. "Marco says *I* healed you," Nick said.

Mr. Herrera chuckled and shook his head. "Well, at least Marco's heart is in the right place."

On the screen the three boys, just a couple of years older, were horseplaying in a park, while Dad tried to control them.

"They're not gonna leave you alone, Nicky. You know that, don't you?" said his father. "At least not for a while."

Nick knew it all too well. He had unleashed more than just a genie from a bottle, and it seemed to be devastating his family as much as it was devastating him. He couldn't bear to see his father like this.

"I'll stop rescuing people," said Nick. "That would make you happy, wouldn't it?" But even as he said it, he knew it made no difference now. He had pushed things too far.

Mr. Herrera took a look at the TV. The three boys tried desperately to make a three-person pyramid, but didn't quite have the balance. "You know what would make me happy?" His father reached out his hand and paused the videotape. "*That* would make me happy," he said, pointing at the frozen image.

Nick knew what he meant. For the first time in his life, Nick wished he was five instead of fifteen — when the toughest problem was figuring out how to tie his own shoelaces.

The creaking of floorboards heralded the arrival of Nick's mother in the room. Nick caught her reflection in the window, but looked away.

She stood there for a moment, waiting. "Look at me, Nicky," she finally said. Nick obeyed. He turned to see his mother's face. It was a strong face that always seemed older so early in the morning. She kept Nick's gaze without blinking, never breaking her hard expression. "Nothing's so bad that you can't look me in the face." She turned and left for the kitchen, to fiddle with the old coffee percolator.

Paulie stumbled into the living room after she left, and threw himself on the recliner. Nick should have been flattered; this was perhaps the first time in recorded history that Paulie was up before eight.

"So, Nicky," Paulie said, picking the sleep from his eyes, "I got this zit on my cheek that won't go away. . . . You think you could slap me with those magic fingers?"

"Shut your mouth, Paulie," said Rose-Marie Herrera, from the kitchen. Paulie chuckled at his joke. Their father just watched the video.

When Mom came back into the room, she brought coffee for Dad and hot chocolate for Nick and Paulie, because she refused to admit her boys could possibly be old enough to drink coffee. She watched for a while as everybody sipped. It felt strange, all of them sitting there before the break of dawn. This only happened when they were getting ready for a big trip. Or some relative died at an ungodly hour.

"Nicky," his mom finally said, "maybe you ought to go to church today. Go to confession."

Paulie threw his head back against the recliner. "And what good is that going to do, Ma?"

"It will ease his mind, that's what it will do — so you stay out of it."

"Great," said Paulie. "Great, Nicky, just rattle off a few Hail Marys and it'll all be OK."

"Hey!" said their mother. "You can believe whatever you choose to believe — I've never stopped you. But in this house you have respect for what *I* believe."

"And what do you believe about Nicky, and what people are saying about him, Mama?" asked Paulie.

She took her time before answering him. Nick listened carefully, but made no attempt to involve himself in the conversation.

"I think Nicky asked for too much excitement, and got it," she said. "And now maybe he won't go running into any more burning buildings. That's what I think."

"You still didn't answer the question," demanded Paulie.

Mom glanced over at Nicky. This time *she* looked away.

"If the Lord wants Nicky to be a healer, then he will be one. And if not, then he won't. That's one thing I'm not gonna worry about." And that being her definitive statement on the matter, she turned and headed into the kitchen, as Paulie, exasperated, headed back to his room. Both of them shook their heads as they left, as if each were saying "How do you ever get through to people like that?" Nick suspected neither of them ever would.

Through all of this, Dad sat quietly, wrapped in his

comforter, tuned into nothing but the video. He did not as much as rub his forehead once.

Through the blinds the first light of dawn lit the room in a dim tone to match the glow of the television. That's when Nick heard a distinct sound on the street. The paperboy dumping loads of newspapers on doorsteps. There were thousands of paperboys in the city. Millions of newspapers. If yesterday had been a slow news day, his incident with Max might just have made the main headline; big black letters two inches high on the paper's front page. His father knew that too.

"We don't have to go out today, Nicky," his father offered, once the others were gone. "We can just stay in here and forget about it. Tomorrow too."

"But you got work. . . ."

"I called in sick."

"But I got a math test. . . ."

"Miss it," said his father. "I'll write you a note." He reached over and took the phone off the hook, laying the receiver face-up on the old end table.

The light of the dawn had grown, and now Nick could see his father's eyes more clearly. They were intensely weary, as if he had suddenly decided he'd seen enough and the world had simply become too much of a burden.

"OK, Dad," said Nick. "I'll stay with you for a while."

On the screen Salvatore dived into a pool, and the film roll ended before he came back up.

15 · Day of Reckoning

Judgment Day descended on Nick Herrera with the fury of a hurricane, and he knew hiding from it would do him not a bit of good. And so, when the limousine arrived at his door sometime around noon, Nick dutifully dressed for the day of festivities, and quietly went along. It was no mystery to Nick where the limousine was going.

● ● ●

On the sixty-seventh floor of the eight-sided sapphire-blue crystalline tower, a copy of the news rested on a marble desk half the size of Nick's entire bedroom. The tower was in the low-rise section of town right between midtown and downtown, specifically designed to leave a drastic and unforgettable impression on the New York skyline.

The two-story letters across the top two floors sent out one unmistakable message: LANKO.

"I want you to know I care a great deal about my daughter," said Lanko, as he gazed out of his window at his empire. Nick sat there listening, pretending that there was nothing oppressive or intimidating about being on the top floor of the Lanko Sapphire Pavilion, in the lavish business office of one of the most important and powerful men in the city. "You see, I'm a busy man," he said, and then made a point of telling Nick just how busy he was.

There was a sizable collection of Lanko towers going up in the city, several more in Chicago; there were bids in on five hotels, and millions of dollars moving back and forth among almost as many banks. "I'm on the job, milking every minute out of every day just to keep afloat," he told Nick.

"*But* I always make time for my daughter. I know where she goes, I know how she spends her money," he said. "I even keep track of the people Linda spends her time with."

He pointed to a stack of manila folders on the edge of his otherwise immaculate desk. "You'd be surprised how many unethical people out there would love to take advantage of a girl in Linda's position." Nick wondered what his file looked like, but decided he'd rather not know.

Lanko sat down in his big leather chair. "Although I usually stand back and trust Linda to make decisions for herself," he said, "there comes the occasional time when, for everyone's sake, I feel I must intervene.

"I care a great deal about my daughter," said Lanko again, leaning forward for emphasis. "And my daughter," Lanko added, "cares a great deal about you. Therefore, I care about you as well. And that's why I'm giving you this." Lanko handed Nick an envelope.

"It's a belated Christmas present," he said. "I was out of town over the holidays, and I wanted to make sure I gave it to you. Perhaps you could use it to put your brother in a better convalescent home," said Lanko. "As it is, it's dangerous for your family to be keeping him at King's County illegally — your father being a policeman and all."

Nick wondered how he knew about that. Linda certainly hadn't told him — according to Linda, she never told her father anything — but he knew, and it made Nick wonder what else Lanko knew about him and his family.

"Thank you," said Nick, putting the envelope into his shirt pocket. Lanko seemed pleased that Nick had accepted it. The man leaned back in his black leather chair and swiveled slightly to the left, then slightly to the right.

"What I tell you now," said Lanko, "is something I've given a great deal of thought to. Please take none of it personally."

Lanko spoke clearly with slick charm. He could have charmed a snake out of its skin. Nick already felt his own skin starting to crawl.

"I've given this careful consideration," he said, "and I've come to realize that you and Linda aren't really good for one another."

Nick swallowed to clear his throat and tried to speak with the force of a man standing his ground. "Are you asking me not to see her anymore?"

"No," said Lanko. "I wouldn't do that. That's your decision to make. Your decision completely."

"Well, I won't stop seeing her!" said Nick.

Lanko didn't react. He just swiveled slightly left, and slightly right, with the cold distance of a winter star.

"Mr. Lanko," said Nick, "if it has to do with that stuff in the news, it's not my fault. I never said I could heal anyone. None of it's true."

"Maybe not," said Lanko. "But it's as true as it needs to be."

"What do you mean?"

"I mean that people have already begun to link your name with the very idea of healing. Whether you can do it or not doesn't matter. In the long run what people think becomes more important than the truth. It *becomes* the truth."

Nick silently took in Lanko's philosophy.

"In any case," said Lanko, "I don't want my daughter mixed up in this sort of thing."

"You can't make me stop seeing her. . . ."

"I told you, I won't make you do anything . . . but after you've weighed both sides, I think you'll reconsider."

Lanko reached into his drawer and pulled out one more manila file folder. "Let me put forth a problem for you to solve," said Lanko, handing the folder to Nick. "Consider it an equation," he said, "an equation I'm leaving for you to balance."

"I'm not good in math," said Nick.

"I know," said Lanko, "but look at the folder."

Nick opened it up slowly. Common sense set off a warning alarm in Nick's head, telling him to leave it on the table, and get up quickly and walk away; stalemate was better than defeat . . . but as usual, curiosity beat out common sense.

The folder was stacked with glossy photos and a legal pad full of notes scribbled in Linda's unmistakably neat handwriting.

"I discovered this file in my daughter's closet this morning," said Lanko. "I found it rather . . . troubling. Do you recognize any of those people?"

Nick didn't feel good about this. Not good at all. "Yeah," said Nick. "This is the guy I pulled from the sewer . . . and this is the girl who was choking at Nathan's. . . ." Nick flipped through the pictures. There were perhaps twenty of them. Among them was the old woman who'd been mugged off-Broadway, and he thought he also recognized one of her muggers.

Nick looked up at Lanko for an explanation, and Lanko raised his eyebrows.

"They're actors," said Lanko. "Every last one of them."

A sense of horror began to fill Nick — a lightheadedness and shortness of breath that had nothing to do with the altitude. Nick closed the file, not wanting to see what was in the perfectly neat notes Linda had so painstakingly written.

Three inexplicably easy rescues.

Linda's change of heart a month ago.

It all made perfect sense now. Nick had been the butt of a rich girl's horrific joke. Max's rescue was the only *true* rescue Nick had performed since his successful stakeout of Central Park. No wonder Linda was so much against his going that night — Max's leap wasn't one of her carefully staged performances. Nick had never felt so betrayed. He had never felt so filthy. Filthier than when he was facedown in the subway slime.

"Take the file with you," said Lanko. "There's some pretty interesting stuff in there. My daughter has a very good imagination."

Nick closed the file and dropped it on the desk, as he stood up. Lanko had won. Nick should have known he would find a way to win, and right now, Nick didn't know who he hated more: the man, or his daughter.

Lanko stood as well, holding out his hand for Nick to shake, but Nick wouldn't.

"I want you to know," said Lanko, "that I *do* like you, Nick. And you can always come to me if you need my help in any way."

"I wanna go," said Nick, like a child waiting to be dismissed. "Can I go now?"

"Let me see you out."

But Nick didn't wait. He left through the large wooden double doors and headed toward the elevator bank.

Mercifully, an elevator opened just as he arrived. For a moment he thought he saw the image of Linda stepping out, wearing one of her sable coats that must have taken the lives of a hundred little animals. For a moment he thought he saw here there, but the elevator was empty.

What would he say to her if she came to his house? What if she called and the phone wasn't off the hook? What then? He wouldn't say anything, he decided. He wouldn't tell her what he knew, he would just push farther and farther away until she got the idea, and left him alone.

Nick stepped into the elevator, and the door closed. His stomach rose to his throat as the floor dropped out beneath him, and the elevator descended, nearly in free fall.

It doesn't matter, he told himself. *Not at all.* But even as he said it, he knew it wasn't true, and he silently wished something awful would happen to Martin Lanko, to make him pay for this cruel afternoon.

As it turned out, Nick's wish was answered remarkably quickly.

16 · Tyrannosaurus Wreck

The crane hadn't been secured as well as it should have been; that much was clear. The whole city knew that Lanko pushed his construction crews to the brink of exhaustion, to keep up his reputation as the city's fastest builder, and his critics complained that Lanko's obsession with speed was bound to affect quality and safety. Somewhere down the line, a bolt would not be tightened; a weld would not be completed; a live electrical wire would be left dangling in the midst of the rush. In short, some people believed that Martin Lanko was an accident waiting to happen. It turned out they were right.

All it took was the hand of the wind sweeping across the thirty-story roof. The immense construction sky-crane began to veer to the right, and the heavy load of steel beams it was hauling up swayed along with it. Then the crane moved left, and its five-ton load swung in the other direction. One row of loose bolts gave way, and then another and then another, as metal fragments flew. The crane careened wildly, dropping its load of steel upon the roof of a car parked on the street. The crash of the steel caused people on the street to scatter instantly. It was the only warning anyone had of what was yet to come.

Across the street, people came to their windows, saw the fleeing workers and pedestrians, and hurried deep into their homes, figuring the whole tower would come toppling down upon their heads.

The crane listed and swung, its controller fighting to steady it as a pilot would fight to land a crippled jet in a thunderstorm. For him, there was no way out as the crane's arm rocked clumsily, like the head of a dying beast, holding, for a brief instant, its last moment of balance.

That's when a car turned onto the street.

The man driving had no concept that what was going on before him was more than just normal construction chaos. He hadn't heard the crashing steel beams, for his stereo was turned up just a touch too loud.

When the crane finally went, it went quickly. The white steel spine that ran the full height of the building tore away from the tower and snapped, sending the unwieldy monster down to its end.

It hit ten floors on the way down, taking out tons of royal-blue marble, pale pink glass, tons of concrete, and the lives of two workers.

Meanwhile, on the ground, the unlucky motorist drummed his steering wheel to the beat of the Rolling Stones, as his car drove into the shadow of the tower.

The sky came down upon his head with no warning, smashing his car as if it were tinfoil, trapping him semiconscious beneath the shattered roof.

The beast lurched, another slab of concrete fell from the building, and finally the beast died. For a moment, the Rolling Stones rambled on about getting some satisfaction, until they finally died as well.

Lanko had six buildings still under construction in the city, and the roll of the dice had brought this particular event to Lanko Terrace Tower, Second Avenue and Ninety-fifth.

Disaster had finally fallen upon Nick's doorstep . . . and Nick was nowhere to be found.

• • •

But Marco was.

• • •

Although Nick had raced from the scene of Max's aborted diving exhibition the night before, Marco had not. He became a disciple, rising to fill the void. Even as Marco's eye swelled with the pain of Nick's punch, he told the press what he knew, painting for the city's mass media the picture of Nick: a reluctant saint, and humble prophet. The press ate it up.

Marco was a fine disciple, for what he lacked in the way of speaking skills he made up for in passion. By morning, Marco was a celebrity in his own right — and for everyone who scoffed and called him an idiot, there was someone else who believed him. Or at least wanted to believe him.

At school, with Nick nowhere to be found, Marco happily found himself the center of attention. By noon kids with everything from asthma to acne began to crowd around him, wanting to know the truth, wanting to know exactly what Nick Herrera might be able to do for them. Marco was more than happy to tell them.

When school let out at 2:45 that day, Marco had, like the Pied Piper, assembled a group of kids who followed him toward the subway. The word was out that Nicky Herrera was giving audiences to the sick, the disabled, and just the curious. Whether they believed he could heal them or not, it was certainly worth the five dollars Marco was charging for admission.

Marco already reckoned himself a rich man, with about one hundred dollars in his pocket, and pledges of almost two hundred more.

Although he hadn't consulted Nick in this little endeavor, he knew Nick would approve once he came around. It was only a matter of Nick adjusting to his new situation — his true calling in life — and all Nick had to do was see the crowds waiting for him. Dozens of people in need with their hands stretched out, reaching toward him. How couldn't Nick be thrilled by that? It would have thrilled Marco.

Marco left the Ninety-sixth Street subway station with his entourage behind him, expecting about twenty more kids to show up later in the day with their sick grandparents, or whatever.

But when they reached Ninety-fifth Street, Marco came face to face with Nick's next great rescue.

It must have happened just before school let out. It must have been loud and it must have been horrible.

Marco's first reaction was awe, and amazement. The kind of feeling he got watching a movie when something particularly destructive happens.

His second reaction was fear, and he raced toward the wreckage, wondering who on his block, if anyone, had been killed.

The rescue effort was well organized and in full swing, but it still seemed to be frenzied. Dozens of rescue workers struggled to dismantle the frame of the crane that lay upon the broken street like the skeleton of a great dinosaur.

Nick's father was there, helping in the rescue. News crews were broadcasting live.

It didn't take long for Marco to find out that several workers had been killed, and so far they'd been able to find one survivor — some guy who was trapped in his car beneath tons of steel and concrete. They were trying desperately to reach him in time, getting closer by the minute, but they still seemed hours away. The twisted wreckage was like a maze, and the workers were using brute force to attack the mess, as if they were digging a tunnel through a mountain. Bit by bit they dismantled whole sections of metal and concrete, and carried it away. They said the wreckage was too unstable for anyone to climb in through one of the many openings. One wrong move and the whole thing would collapse.

But this was not the way to go about saving this man. What they needed was someone willing to risk death by climbing deep into the unstable wreckage and pulling out the injured man.

What they needed was Nick.

Marco ran to find his fearless friend, but he was

not home. Nor was he in the street, and neither of Nick's parents could say where he was. But Marco knew Nick would be there any minute, and so he waited, watching the workers' futile attempts to reach the lone survivor.

• • •

By four o'clock, Marco began to worry. Nick was still not there, and it was making both of them look very, very bad. Marco had spent an hour telling his friends gathered around him — and anyone else who would listen — that they were all about to get a once-in-a-lifetime chance to see the master at work. They would get to witness Nick performing a rescue that no one else could.

Marco imagined the rest of the crowd that had gathered was waiting for Nicky as well. He imagined the rescue workers and the news crews were waiting for him. To Marco, the whole world awaited the arrival of Nicholas Herrera.

But what if Nicky didn't show?

It was this unhappy thought that set off a chain reaction in Marco's mind, bringing him closer and closer to a decision he never dreamed he'd have the privilege to make.

If Nicky didn't show, then someone else would have to perform this job.

Marco began to consider things seriously. How closely was Marco tied in to Nicky's special abilities? Was Marco just Nick's friend, or was he also Nick's accomplice? Kind of like Batman and Robin. Were they partners?

True, Marco hadn't been there for all of Nick's

rescues, but he *had* been there for the most important ones. Marco *did* take the call from the leaper. Marco *was* quoted in the news. He *had* gathered the crowds.

Certainly Marco couldn't heal, but this was different. It was easier. And who knew, maybe some of Nicky had rubbed off on Marco, like static on a balloon. Maybe, if Marco performed his own rescue, he could earn membership into the elite class of girls who were filthy rich, and boys who could fly. Perhaps then someone like Linda Lanko could stand to be in the same room with him.

Marco knew only one way to find out whether he should or shouldn't take Nick's place.

Marco reached into his back pocket and found a coin.

Holding his breath, he flipped it high into the air, as he always saw Nick do. He flipped it only once — once was all he believed he needed. The coin came down and he slapped it to the back of his hand, slowly taking his other hand away to reveal Thomas Jefferson's profile. He had his answer.

• • •

The rescue workers had all filed out of the structure. They seemed to have stopped, or were taking a break. They hung around, mumbling to each other and shaking their heads, not too happy about things. Marco took this as his opportunity to seize the day.

Without thinking twice, Marco jumped the barricade and raced through the police like a wide receiver dodging across the field for a touchdown. In moments he was climbing the twisted wreckage, ignoring the warning shouts behind him as he slipped in through the many holes of the dead iron dinosaur.

Marco climbed like a champion — just as Nick would have — with his heart pounding and his blood filled with adrenaline. He moved deeper and deeper, squeezing through hollows and cavities no one else dared to, until he reached the crushed shell of the car.

He stuck his head through the broken window, and found the survivor. . . .

. . . Only this guy wasn't a survivor anymore.

And it dawned on Marco that this was the reason the rescue workers were taking a break. Suddenly there was no more rush. It didn't matter anymore how long it took to get him out.

As if unable to contain its laughter, the dead beast around him shrugged, sending out a thunderclap the likes of which Marco had never heard . . . and Marco knew, even before the steel beam came crashing down upon him, that his sudden luck had come to a sudden end.

17 · *Tails*

Nick had forgotten how easy it was to disappear in the city — how easy it was to find perfect solitude by surrounding himself with thousands of strangers. After escaping Martin Lanko's office of horrors, Nick headed downtown, away from home and everyone he knew. In his parka, scarf, and woolen hat, he was unrecognizable, almost invisible.

Two hours later, Nick found himself emerging from the towers of New York's financial district, into Battery Park, at the very southern tip of the long thin island of Manhattan, and he made his way through the trees and stone slab monoliths filled with the names of the war dead. He made his way down to the edge of New York Harbor, gripping onto the railing tightly, as if letting go would cause him to be sucked back home in an instant.

A meager group of sightseers boarded the last ferry to the Statue of Liberty, fighting the wind as they hurried onto the deck. Nick would have gone with them, just to get farther and farther away, but the nickel and three pennies he had in his pocket would not pay his passage to Liberty Island. In the end, he knew he would have to go back. There was no escape.

He looked at his glove-covered hands. They were ordinary hands. Linda knew that. And yet she had feared them so much that she had to tie them up with false rescues. He thought he understood why, but it didn't make it hurt any less. Now she had him so confused, he no longer could be certain of his own abilities to rescue people, and he could never forgive Linda for that.

Salvatore had been right, the bastard. You can't trust anybody, and nobody gives you anything for free. Life's a bitch and then you die. Salvatore had been right, and Nick hated him for it. He didn't know who he hated more, Salvatore, Lanko, or his daughter.

At 4:30, as the day began to wane, Nick turned around for the long walk home, a trip that would take him at least three hours. He could stretch it out to four if he walked slowly.

Nick didn't hear the news until he passed an appliance store at the edge of the park — and when he saw it, he didn't see it once, but a dozen times, on twelve television screens in the window, each broadcasting in perfect, horrifying clarity. They gave Nick a fragmented, insect's-eye view of the live news report.

Rescue workers sawed away the gnarled metal girders, as if carefully dismantling a house of cards ... and in a moment Nick recognized everything: the graffiti on wooden construction partitions across the street, the fire hydrant that someone had painted red, white, and blue, the cars parked on the street.

"What is she saying?" Nick screamed at passersby. "What is she saying?" But no one answered.

Nick ran into the store, and found another bank of televisions even larger than the first, all tuned in to the same station. He pulled what he could from the report he heard.

3:15 today. Four dead. Who? Who? Workers. A civilian in a car. A survivor was trapped in the wreckage. A worker. Not a worker — a youth. What the hell did they mean by youth?

At first they thought it was Nick — who else would race into a disaster like a moron? — Then they discovered that it wasn't Nick at all but another neighborhood boy. . . .

Nick knew who it was even before they said the name, and suddenly the distance between home and Battery Park stretched to light-years.

A block away Nick found a subway station and raced down the steps. What did Marco think he was doing? Didn't he know you didn't race blindly into a catastrophe unless you were *meant* to? Nick was the only person experienced enough to do something like that!

Just as the uptown train pulled in, Nick leapt over the turnstile . . . and right into the chest of a very wide cop.

"Where's your token?" said the unyielding cop.

"I got a pass," said Nick. He searched in his pocket for his wallet that contained his subway pass, but he didn't have it. It was on his desk at home.

"I forgot it. . . . This is an emergency — don't you know who I am?"

"I don't care. You ride the subway, you use a token."

Nick didn't have time to explain. He tried to push his way past the cop. The train doors had opened.

The cop held him with an iron grip. "What do you think, you're special?"

The train doors closed and the train began to pull out. Nick did not have time for this.

He raced up the stairs, against the flow of traffic, begging for money that only tourists were likely to give.

•   •   •

Above the station was a small grocery store, and Nick raced in, setting off jingle bells by the door that signaled incoming customers. He looked around wildly. He saw about five customers. Business people mostly.

Even before he said anything, they looked at him as if he were crazy. The way he was breathing, the way his eyes must have looked. He pulled off his cap and his hair was a frazzled mess.

"I need a subway token," he panted, grabbing people by the shoulder and turning them around. "I need it now! Anybody."

He tugged on people's sleeves, but they turned their backs. People farther away ducked down the aisles. So practiced were these city dwellers at dodging incessant panhandlers, they had perfected the art of saying no.

"Just a dollar," pleaded Nick. "For the subway. A dollar."

Nothing.

"Don't you know who I am?"

But apparently no one knew, and no one cared.

It was as if the powers that be were testing him, and what a damn lousy time they had picked for a test.

Then Nick remembered something. He unzipped his coat and pulled an envelope out of his shirt pocket. He tore it open and looked at the check inside with no interest other than its being a means to an end.

"I've got a five-thousand-dollar check from Martin Lanko here!" he said. "I'll give it to anyone who'll give me a dollar!"

If people thought he was crazy before that, now they were certain. They laughed and shook their heads. He could have killed them for it. He could have shot them all dead.

The Korean cashier stood by the register, keeping it closed.

"I need a dollar," Nick said angrily. "Open the cash register."

The cashier shook his head. "No free money," he said in a heavy accent. "You buy something, I give you change. No free money."

"Open the damned register and give me a buck. I got an emergency. I got a dying friend!"

"No!"

Nick leaned forward and banged his shin against the newspaper rack. It hurt, so he kicked the rack. Stupid thing. Damn stupid thing. Friggin' stupid thing.

Anyone who'd been brave enough to stay near the counter this long was already either leaving, or moving to a safe distance. There was no telling what could happen in situations like this.

"Just open the register!"

"No!"

"Do it!"

"I call police!"

Nick didn't have time to argue; he was a man with a mission and needed a quick means of persuasion. He employed the first thing that came to mind.

"Open the friggin' register or I'll beat the hell out of you, I swear I will!"

The few onlookers backed farther away into the recesses of the store.

"Do it!" screamed Nick.

If this worked, Nick decided he would take five dollars. Ten. Enough to get him a cab home, which would probably be faster than the subway. Twenty just to piss the guy off. Fifty. He deserved that. He deserved more than that, for he was a man with a mission. Couldn't they see that?

The stone face of the Korean merchant did not change. He reached down beneath the counter and pulled out a small shiny black object. The man had been through this many times before and was damn tired of it. Someone would pay. He shakily aimed the gun at Nick, saying nothing.

And suddenly Nick knew that this was not a test at all. This was a man. With a gun. Aimed at his face.

"No!"

Nick reacted quickly, instinctively throwing both hands out in front of him to block the bullet.

What happened next went so quickly that witnesses would never agree as to what really took place.

A woman entered the door.

The sight of the gun made her scream.

The sound of the scream made the grocer flinch.
The force of the flinch made the gun go off.
The blast of the gun made Nick dodge to the left.
But he wasn't fast enough.
He just wasn't fast enough.
And it only took an instant for all the lights shining in his face to flip over into darkness.

18 · *These Hands*

At dawn, the towers of Manhattan take the sun and fragment it into a million different reflections, bouncing back and forth on the smooth glass faces, until no one knows where the sun really is.

To the brownstones that face Lanko Sapphire Pavilion, the sun is blue and rises in the west.

To the Fifth Avenue apartments that face the jagged, crystalline face of Trump Tower, there are six suns, all dim bronze, that rise in the north.

And to the frantic executives who haunt the narrow roads around Wall Street, the sun never does seem to rise at all.

If you try to find the morning light in the many reflections, you may never find an image that is true, and if you try to see yourself, the distorted faces you get can make you forget which one is real.

But, for once, Nicholas Herrera did not need to worry about this. He did not see any reflections today. He did not see the sunrise.

Nick was awake, but not awake; aware, but unaware, as he lay in a bed on a high floor of the white gothic tower of New York Hospital. Whatever drug they had pumped into him was doing a damn good job of numbing every inch of his body with a warm weightless sensation.

The curtains were drawn, blocking out the sun. His father slept in a chair beside him. His mother slept in the hospital waiting room. Nick couldn't read a comic book to pass the time, because his arms were covered in bandages from the tip of his fingers almost to his elbows.

Nick had not been successful in blocking the grocer's bullet with his hands. It had pierced the palm of his right, shattered the wrist of his left, then veered east and embedded in his right shoulder.

Nick hadn't felt much pain, because he had wisely passed out the moment he saw the blood. But he knew it would be waiting for him when the painkiller wore off.

The doctor had said, in the midst of everything, that Nick was truly lucky — that if the bullet had been of a higher caliber, he would have no hands left to bandage.

Nick was too tired to wonder whether it was good luck, bad luck, or a confused reflection of some greater design.

• • •

Linda stole up to Nick's room a short time later. She was afraid if she didn't go now she might never have the nerve again — for although nerve was her most valued commodity, she barely had enough of it to face Nick Herrera.

When she had discovered her entire file of actors and list of rescues was gone, she knew her father had found it. She also knew her father well enough to know that he had shown it to Nick. It was simply a Lanko thing to do; Linda knew her father wanted them away from each other, and so he used the best possible means at his disposal. Strictly a business move.

She tried to call Nicky, but his phone was busy all afternoon — most likely off the hook. She tried to call Lanko to tell him he had ruined her life, but he had gone off to some crisis somewhere. There was always some crisis somewhere.

It wasn't until late that evening, when she chanced to turn on the eleven o'clock news, that she received the full measure of what had gone on that day —both uptown and downtown.

Nick was shot while robbing a store.

Marco had been trapped by a construction crane.

And even as the news unfolded before her eyes, and her heart seized with shock, she could not stop thinking how, in many respects, she was responsible for both events.

And so visiting Nick took every last ounce of nerve she had.

• • •

Linda waited in the shadows of the hallway, watching until Nick's father left the room. She did not want to see him. She needed time alone with Nick. Time to talk to him, to explain to him. To keep the words flowing until she gained his confidence once more. She had no specific plan, but she knew one would come.

Nick was awake but groggy as she stepped into the dark room. His eyes rested at half-mast, and he did not react to her. Either he didn't see her, or wasn't surprised that she was there, or was too drugged to care. His hands were wrapped in so many bandages he looked like a mummy.

"Nick?" said Linda, quietly.

"How's Marco?" were the first weak words out of his mouth. "Everyone keeps telling me he's OK, and I shouldn't worry about that now, but no one looks me in the eye." Nick finally turned his droopy eyes to hers. "How's Marco?"

Linda wouldn't lie to him. He'd heard enough lies from her to last a lifetime. "Marco's *not* OK," said Linda quietly. Nick closed his eyes and took a slow, deep breath. His feet moved just a bit. He opened his eyes to half-moons again.

"Is he dead?" Nick asked.

Linda shook her head. "He's downstairs." Linda had peeked in at Marco before she came up. He did not look good, and Linda couldn't bear the sight for more than an instant. "They don't know, Nicky. He's got internal bleeding, and his leg is . . . well, part of the crane came down on his leg. He was under there for hours. . . ."

Linda searched her brain for something positive to say. "But," she said hopefully, "he made it through the first night, and that's always the hardest."

"Will he lose his leg?" asked Nick.

Again Linda fought the urge to lie. "Maybe," said Linda. "Probably. They won't know for a while."

Nick didn't say anything for a long time. She had expected him to curse at her, or yell at her or spit at her or something, and she had all her defenses worked out. *I staged those rescues to protect you,* she would say, *and besides there were only three of them,* she would add. She could go on and on, making herself sound blameless, and if she tried really hard, she might allay her own growing guilt.

But Nick didn't want to talk about that. He reached lazily for the nurse's call button, but his bandaged hands couldn't push it. Linda didn't help him. She did not want any nurse barging in and ruining everything.

Finally Nick asked a simple question. "What floor am I on? I don't know what floor I'm on. I don't even know what hospital this is."

"New York Hospital," said Linda, and Nick seemed instantly relieved. "Twelfth floor."

And then he was quiet again. She couldn't stand it.

"I want you to know," she said, "that my father is paying Marco's medical bills. He'll have the finest care he can get. The best doctors."

"That's good," said Nick.

"And," she said, thinking about it for the first time, and committing herself to it at the very moment, "I'm setting up a fund for Marco. I've decided." She began to pace through the room, setting her new equation into action. "I'll start it with my own money, and then get donations from around the city. I know lots of people — we can make it a big deal, and Marco can come out rich."

"Maybe he can buy himself a new leg," said Nick.

But Linda refused to hear that. "I'm paying for *your* medical expenses, too," said Linda. "Out of my own pocket. I've decided, so don't try to talk me out of it." She paced to the window and opened the curtains. Yes, she knew what to do. It would be easy. "And we can make that whole business about the robbery stuff, we can make it go away. It was probably just a misunderstanding anyway."

"Linda," said Nick, his half-moon eyes never changing. "Linda," he said, "go away."

Linda stopped pacing and looked at Nick. This was unexpected, not in the plans. Nick didn't seem angry, so she couldn't defend herself. He didn't seem weepy, so she couldn't comfort him. He just seemed . . . tired.

"Nick, I want to make things better. I can do it. Give me a chance."

"Linda," Nick said slowly, and calmly, "you can do whatever you want with your money; I don't care. But there's some stuff you just can't buy." Nick lifted his hand and tried to push the call button again.

"Nick," she said, "I know you don't mean that. You're just saying that because you're upset and you're hurt and . . ."

"No, Linda," he said. "I'm saying it 'cause it's true. I'm sorry," he said. "I'm really sorry." Nick tried again to hit the call button, grimaced, and finally gave up, so he closed his eyes and waited. He waited for her to go away.

Linda stood there, her perfect plan shattered. Nick wasn't going to say anything more about it, and for the first time she could remember, all Linda's words left her. For the first time she could remember, she had lost.

"I'll send in the nurse," she said. Linda turned and

strode out, her fur coat of one hundred skins flowing behind her like a thick, soft cape.

After getting the nurse, Linda headed straight for the elevators, the anger fermenting inside her. How dare he? How dare he ruin her perfect plan? Who did he think he was? She could have done it! She could have!

And all at once her face began to flush in confusion.

No matter how smoothly she could palm it all off onto him — blaming him for pushing her away at a time of crisis — the honest truth was that she had used him. However good her intentions, she had toyed with him and manipulated him, just as she had done with everyone in her life, for as long as she could remember — and no matter how good the two of them were together, what good was it when she insisted on having Nick on a string?

Nick could lose his hands. Marco could lose his life. What good could any of her manipulations and equations do them now? Something inside her would have to change — but she did not know where to begin.

As she stepped in the empty elevator, she began to wonder. Had she ever offered Nick anything besides money? Besides games and carefully balanced equations? Did she have anything else inside her to give?

And she cried because she did not know.

• • •

The time of running was over. Nick was too tired to run — too tired of hearing everyone else's mind without taking the time to make up his own. If he was still up on that ledge with Max, then it was time to come down.

"*Everything happens for a reason,*" his mother had said.

"*Max is crazy and Marco's an imbecile,*" Linda had said.

"*What other people believe becomes the truth,*" Lanko had said. If Nick heard another opinion, he'd blow up.

A nurse came, poured him some water, then left. Once she was gone, Nick forced himself out of bed and made his way down the hall to the elevator bank.

As the elevator dropped floor by floor, Nick felt his hands and shoulder begin to throb with fire. The morphine must have been wearing off.

His timing was exceptional. As he stepped out of the elevator, the two nurses at the intensive care desk were too busy to bother with him, and so, with hands hidden behind his back, Nick sauntered through without being questioned.

Marco was attached to half a dozen machines. His face was bruised and scratched. He had a black eye, and it took a moment for Nick to remember that Nick had inflicted the black eye himself.

Marco's leg was wrapped in more bandages than Nick's hands were and was in a double splint, probably because it was still too swollen to put in a cast.

And Nick cried for Marco, for the luck he never had. Perhaps Nick got just what he had coming to him — but Marco's only crime was his faith in Nick. He deserved better than this.

With his teeth, Nick undid the tape around his right hand, and slowly, layer after layer, he unwound the white gauze until a red-brown spot appeared.

The spot grew larger with each layer, and brighter red, until the gauze pulled fully away, revealing an oozing spider of black stitches across his bloated hand. It felt raw and sensitive, and the air around it seemed to have the sharpest of teeth. He dared not move his fingers.

He carefully undid his other hand in the same way. Then he looked at his hands, as he grimaced from the pain.

He hesitated for a moment, and, closing his eyes, he said a silent and simple prayer.

Then, swallowing a scream, Nick pressed his swollen hands firmly against Marco's broken body.

19 · Scars and Cocoons

Lanko Terrace Tower suffered just enough damage to put its completion date five months behind schedule. On the royal-blue marble cornerstone there was a plaque listing the names of those killed in the accident.

But other than that, those names were forgotten.

Just like the other names that popped in and out of the news every day.

Just like Max Barbett, who survived open-heart surgery, and vanished into the same obscurity he had endured before being on the cover of *Time* magazine twice.

Just like Nicholas Herrera.

•   •   •

On the first Saturday in June, Nick found himself sitting in an old, cluttered office that distinctly reminded him of the principal's office at school — an office that, over the years, Nick had become quite familiar with.

But this was his first time in *this* particular office.

The woman behind the desk mumbled to herself as she browsed through the various papers Nick had brought with him, and the various forms he had just filled out. She paused only to take the occasional suck on her cigarette.

"Have you ever done this sort of work before?" she asked.

"No," Nick had to admit.

She threw him a dubious gaze, then returned her eyes to the files and forms.

Nick subconsciously began to scratch the scars on his hands. All that was left of the pain now was an itch. It used to wake him up at nights, but now it just bothered him every once in a while. He flexed his hands and felt the knotty scars. He could flex them pretty well now, and move his fingers about — although he would never be playing the piano.

Nick's wounds had taken forever to heal, becoming infected and reinfected, month after month. His bandages stayed on through the rest of winter and most of spring.

With the bandages on, Nick found it hard to do much of anything, much less flip a coin mindlessly while waiting for a train, and when the bandages finally came off, he was broken of that lifelong habit.

Marco, on the other hand, was much luckier. The swelling in his leg went down quickly, and the shattered bone fragments found their proper locations with the first set. Marco spent three weeks in traction, then two months in a wheelchair. He was now undergoing rehabilitation, and was doing surprisingly well. It looked as though he would emerge with a minimum of permanent damage, if any.

"It sometimes happens that way," the doctors had told him and his family. "Some people heal better and faster than others." Superior genes, they had said.

But Marco had his own theory.

"You know what *I* think?" Marco had said to Nick, shortly after he had gotten out of traction.

Nick had smiled. "Yeah, Marco, I know what you think." And that was all that was said. They understood each other perfectly, and Marco never again brought up the topic of healing after that.

Across the worn aluminum desk, the smoking woman stacked the papers before her in a neat pile, flicked her long ash into an overstuffed tray, let out a hacking cough, then looked up at Nick.

"You probably could make more money," suggested the woman, "if you went back to working at McDonald's this summer."

"There's no future in food service," said Nick. "Not for me, anyway."

The woman smiled, apparently approving of Nick's response.

"Why is it that you want to work in a hospital?" she asked him. "Being an orderly is not a fun summer job."

"I thought it would be a good experience."

"Do you want a career in the health profession?"

"Yeah," Nick admitted. "Maybe a paramedic."

The woman raised her eyebrows, a bit surprised. "Not a doctor?"

Nick shrugged, smiling politely. "My grades aren't the best."

The woman looked down at the pile before her, and pulled out Nick's various report cards, holding them like an oversized poker hand as she examined them.

"Well, you're not exactly the top of your class," she said, "but you're having a very good semester." She eyed Nick, examining him, or judging him, or reading his mind, or whatever it is that hospital personnel officers do.

"You should have more faith in yourself, Mr. Herrera," she said.

Nick could only smile at that. Right now he was just taking it one step at a time. Yes, he knew his being a doctor was a long shot, but she was right; it was possible. If he could get a B+ in math, anything was possible.

"I'm curious," said the woman, "as to why you chose King's County. There are lots of hospitals closer to where you live."

"My brother's here," Nick answered simply.

"He works here?"

"No," said Nick, "he's a patient. Long-term."

"Oh," said the woman. She shifted uncomfortably in her chair, coughed a few times, and mercifully put out her cigarette.

Actually Nick didn't need this interview to get the job. He could have gone through his uncle Steve, who was a big shot at King's County. But Nick didn't want special treatment. He hadn't even told his parents about this yet — they thought he was out playing ball. Not that he lied to his parents much anymore — he just wanted this to be a surprise.

After he was shot, it was as if Nick had started all over with his parents from scratch. Because of the bandages, they cut his meat for him and fed him as if he were a baby. They took such care and had such patience, Nick could not harbor any resentment or feel any embarrassment about his predicament — even when Paulie teased that he ought to have a high chair.

They rarely spoke at home of his rescues, and when they did, they talked calmly, as if it were all ancient history — the good and the bad. "You've got a lot to be proud of," his mother had told him. "But I'll kill you if you try it again!"

His family helped him through those first months, just as they had sat by Salvatore's side, at first. And finally, when the bandages came off his hands, it was as if Nick had come out of a cocoon. The world now seemed a much saner and much more inviting place — the type of place where he could think of the future without fear of being left behind, or closed in.

"Thank you," said the woman across the desk, as she prepared to light another cigarette. "You'll hear from us by next week." And then she added, "I don't think you have to worry about it."

As Nick got up to leave, the woman stopped him.

"Don't I . . . know you from somewhere?" she asked. "Your face seems very familiar."

"Naah," said Nick. "People always say that. I guess I must look like a lot of people."

• • •

Up on King's County's fifth floor, Nick took his time walking down the hall — not because he didn't want to be there, but because he was in no great hurry. He had all the time in the world today. He had planned to visit Salvatore before he left the hospital, and now he was actually looking forward to it.

The numbers passed by on his left: 515, 517, 519.

The last time he had been here, Linda had been with him. The thought of her now made his spirit sway just a bit. Nick occasionally saw Linda's picture in the papers. She was dating the son of some big movie producer, and the gossip tabloids wouldn't leave her alone. It was not a pleasant way to live.

Although there were other girls Nick was dating, for the longest time, he had wanted to call Linda — to ask her if this guy she was seeing was just a flake, or was he for real, and did she take him up to the grid?

But the urge to call her slowly went away.

Perhaps someday Nick would be a skilled physician and would get to treat Linda for ulcers and migraine headaches. Maybe then they could fall in love again.

523 . . . 525 . . . 527 . . .

Salvatore's door was only a few yards down now. Nick picked up his pace just a bit, but then hesitated at the threshold.

Although he really wasn't thinking much about it, a thought had been playing in and out of his mind for a few weeks now. It was a tiny whisper of "what if. . . ." The thought tickled him, but not much more.

529.

Nick pushed open the door, and walked right in.

There were no flowers in the room this time. It didn't smell as fresh as it did on Sal's birthday, but that was all right. Nick had no hate left for Salvatore now — and fear had been replaced by an understanding. Salvatore, Nick realized, was a lot like him — but unlike Nick, Sal had never come out of his cocoon — and although by birthdays, Salvatore was twenty-five and Nick was sixteen, Nick felt like the older brother.

"Hi, Sal," Nick said. He sat down beside his brother, but didn't touch him. Not yet.

Sure, after everything, Nick had no reason to believe he could heal. Everything could be explained. Everything could *always* be explained. But now, it didn't seem to matter anymore, for either way, Nick's plans were not going to change. He had a good sense of what he wanted in life. And he believed in himself just enough to know that it wasn't completely out of his reach.

Nick reached down and took Salvatore's hand, wrapping his own stiff fingers around his brother's. For an instant Nick felt something pass between them. It could have been static electricity, or just a sense of relief.

Nick smiled. Perhaps, like the many doctors and nurses who had attended to his brother, Nick would not be able to heal him . . .

. . . But if he could, he'd have so many things to tell Salvatore!